Ty saw Bri crouch down beside his little girl.

She'd also removed her shoes, he realized, surprised by the move. Her pants were rolled up past her knees and she, too, dabbled in the water.

He walked over slowly, enjoying the picture of the two of them, so fair against the vivid water. They could have passed for mother and daughter.

As fast as it came, Ty thrust the thought away, anger burning in a tight hot spot deep inside. His daughter didn't have a mother. God had taken her away in some kind of cruel divine joke. Fine, he'd deal with that. But no one, including an aunt who made him feel things he shouldn't, was going to part him from his little girl.

He'd play the hand he was given. Alone.

Books by Lois Richer

Love Inspired

LOIS RICHER

lives in a small Canadian prairie town with her husband, who, she says, is a "wanna-be farmer." She began writing in self-defense, as a way to escape. She says, "Come spring, tomato plants take over my flower beds, no matter how many I 'accidentally' pull up or 'prune.' By summer I'm fielding phone calls from neighbors who don't need tomatoes this fall. Come September, no one visits us and anyone who gallantly offers to take a box invariably ends up with six. I have more recipes with tomatoes than with chocolate. Thank goodness for writing! Imaginary people with imaginary gardens are much easier to deal with!"

Lois is pleased to present this latest book in her series, IF WISHES WERE WEDDINGS, for the Steeple Hill Love Inspired line. Please feel free to contact Lois at: Box 639, Nipawin, Saskatchewan, Canada S0E 1E0.

Blessed Baby
Lois Richer

™ *Love Inspired*®

Published by Steeple Hill Books™

STEEPLE HILL BOOKS

Steeple
Hill™

ISBN 0-373-87159-7

BLESSED BABY

Copyright © 2001 by Lois Richer

This edition published by arrangement with Steeple Hill Books.

Visit us at www.steeplehill.com

Printed in U.S.A.

Before they call, I will answer.
And while they are still speaking, I will hear.
—*Isaiah* 65:24

This book is for two blessed babies—C and J.
May you never outgrow your dreams.

Chapter One

"It's fifteen months too late, but I'm here, Bridget."

Briony Green brushed away a tear of remembrance, the whispered words echoing through her car. Reluctantly she tore her gaze away from the rugged mountains of Banff, still snow-capped in June.

It was time.

Bri parked on the side street marked Bear, searching for the address. It wasn't that she *wanted* to do this, she *had* to. She owed it to her sister.

She counted down the numbers. There it was—a pretty stone cottage. Number 132. According to her information this was the place.

"Oh, Lord, please help me," she murmured, scrunching her eyes closed as she drew a deep breath of courage.

Then, with the resolute determination Bri applied to every difficult task she undertook, she climbed out of her car, walked up to the solid oak door and gave two hard raps.

The man who pulled open the door wore a blue

flowered apron spattered with a variety of foods. That feminine bit of cloth did absolutely nothing to diminish the masculinity of his lean tanned face. His chocolate-brown hair stood up in wild tufts, adding to his craggy manliness.

He was *not* what she'd expected.

"Yes?" He waited impatiently for Bri to state her business. A quick glance over one shoulder indicated his harried state.

It was obvious to Bri that she'd interrupted his dinner.

"Are you Tyrel Demens?" Briony's voice scraped out in a nervous squawk.

"Yes." His brows lowered fractionally, his attention concentrated on her fully now.

Briony huffed out a sigh of relief. At least she had the right house. Now for the hard part.

"My name is Briony Green," she told him, offering a tentative smile.

He didn't smile back.

"I understand you have a daughter, Mr. Demens."

The glower hardened into an outright frown as suspicion swirled in his brown stare. In one all-consuming assessment, his gaze took in her plain face, her ordinary blue pantsuit and the handbag she clutched against her stomach to stop the nerves.

Reaction was immediate. Eyes narrowed, darkened to coal chips. Lips pinched tight. Hands bunched at his sides.

"What do you want?"

"I think—no, I'm certain that I'm your daughter's aunt," she blurted out, eager to remove the worry from his face.

A wail from inside the house diverted his attention for just a moment.

"I can see you're busy," she offered, fidgeting from one foot to the other. "And I really don't want to intrude. It's just that Bridget, my sister, never told us she'd had a baby."

"Look, I haven't got time—" The wails were getting louder now.

"Please, just hear me out."

Oh, how she longed to be back in her lab! At least there, she was alone, comfortable. Here, she was butting into this man's house, interrupting his day. The big man towered over her, brimming with tension. It was obvious he longed to ignore her by slamming the door. Bri couldn't let that happen.

"I'm keeping you from something and I'm really sorry. It's just that with Bridget gone, I felt it was my duty to make sure her daughter was well taken care of." She stopped, worried herself now by the high-pitched sobs she could hear. "I just wanted to assure myself that the child is all right—"

The unmistakable sound of shattering glass cut through the words. Briony's voice died away as the man in front of her wheeled around, his attention elsewhere. His low rumbly voice brooked no argument.

"Wait here. I'll be right back."

She stepped backward into the porch, watched as he closed and locked the door carefully behind him. Through a pane of etched glass, muffled voices from the other room drifted toward her. She could hear Mr. Demens's low soothing tone and the softer voice of a woman. His wife?

Determined not to eavesdrop, Briony couldn't help seeing what was in front of her. She glanced through the glass, assessing, filing away details. It was a small kitchen, homey with its flowering window plants and bright yellow walls. It could have been pretty, but the mess made her wince. Dishes strewn everywhere; pots piled high in the sink; plates and glasses on the table; an open loaf of bread on the counter. Stains and spills obscured the floor.

The entire room set her back teeth jangling. Surely a little organization couldn't hurt.

A minute later, Tyrel sauntered back into the kitchen carrying a small child clad only in a diaper. With one hand he snicked the lock off and tugged open the door.

"Sorry. When Cristine calls, she doesn't like to be ignored, especially after a nap." He waved Briony inside.

"Is she all right? I heard the glass break." Though she searched, Briony could see nothing to indicate injury on that pale, perfect baby skin. Gingerly she stepped over the threshold.

"Oh, Cristine's fine. Getting more active every day. She reached out from her crib and managed to knock a lamp on the floor. I'll have to move things around again." He brushed his lips against the glossy gold curls and smiled. "This is my daughter." His pride was unmistakable.

Briony's breath snagged in her throat as saucer-wide blue eyes winked down at her from the security of Tyrel's wide football shoulders. She didn't need blood tests or any formal papers to identify the mother of this child. She could see Bridget in the small tilted nose, the firmly pointed chin, the long, slender fingers.

Cristine Demens *was* Bridget's daughter.

"Now, you were saying something about your sister?"

He stood silent, playing with the little girl's fingers as Briony explained how she'd found her sister's diary—about the words that had shocked her parents.

"We had no idea she was going to have a baby, you see. We knew nothing about her life before she came home." Briony tried to explain her sister's tumultuous existence in as few details as possible.

"She ran away, demanded to be left alone. She only returned a few months before she died. She said she needed a place to crash. By then she was so ill we didn't dare question her about her past."

"And you believe Cristine is your sister's baby?" He frowned, obviously not happy with the idea.

Bri nodded. "I'm almost certain she is. I found this tucked inside the cover of Bridget's diary." She held out the legal paper by which Bridget Green had forfeited all rights to her daughter. Some nagging memory twigged at her brain.

"But you must have known Bridget," she murmured, studying the confusion on his face. She reviewed the sheet in one quick glance. "A Mrs. Andrea Demens signed this paper."

Tyrel stared at her, glanced down at the paper for one interminable second, then shook his head in a firm, decisive jerk. "That's impossible! The adoption was closed. We weren't allowed to know the birth mother."

Briony thought for a moment. "Isn't Andrea Demens your wife?" she asked softly, and wondered at the stark despair that immediately washed over his face.

"She was. She died over a year ago."

"I'm so sorry." The pinched lines around his eyes

deepened, and Bri wished suddenly that she hadn't probed.

"It's all right." Tyrel turned away to tuck his daughter into her high chair, then handed her a biscuit. He waited until she began gnawing at it, he turned back to Briony. His face blanched a chalky white. "May I see that again? Please?"

She handed over the document, puzzled by his words. How could he not know? Bridget wrote that she'd studied the family very carefully before she'd agreed to give up her child.

Tyrel Demens was a tall man, six feet at least. He appeared exactly as she'd expected a forest ranger to look: lean, muscular, powerful. But more than that, he seemed completely capable of any challenge fatherhood could bring.

What Briony hadn't expected was the glint of hurt she saw lingering in his eyes.

He studied the signatures at the bottom with an intensity that frightened Bri. Was he going to dispute her claim, pretend the signatures were forged? A brooding fear clutched her heart.

She suddenly wished she hadn't felt obligated to do this, hadn't allowed herself to believe she could make it up to Bridget by checking on her baby. Her sister had made a lot of mistakes, but she'd always been a perfect judge of character. She wouldn't have given her child to these people unless she was certain they would make good parents.

"I'm sure it's all quite legal," she murmured, watching the carved lines around his mouth deepen.

"Yes, of course it is. I wouldn't have tolerated anything else where Cristine was concerned." His smile eased the harshness in his voice as he handed back the paper. "I'm sorry. I wasn't questioning you. It's just...strange that I didn't know about this. Andrea said..." His voice died away, leaving an empty silence that stretched between them.

Briony couldn't think of anything to say. There were no words for a situation like this. She stared at him mutely.

He shook his head as if to clear it. "Never mind. It doesn't really matter now, does it?"

"No, you're right," she agreed with a twinge of relief. "The past isn't important. And I haven't come to cause you any problems." She hurried to assure him. "I just wanted a chance to see the baby, to make sure she was well. I felt I owed that to my sister."

"Of course." Every feature altered from protective to adoring as he bestowed a tender smile on his daughter. "Well, here she is. Say hello, Cris. This is your aunt—" He turned to look at Briony. "I'm sorry, I've forgotten your name."

"Briony Green. Auntie Bri," she murmured, bending to meet the child on her own level. "Hello, sweetheart," she whispered, tentatively stretching out one hand to touch the fair silky skin. Cristine studied her aunt very seriously for a moment, then she grinned, her baby teeth shining proudly out between her chubby lips. She reached to curve her fingers around Bri's.

"Up," she demanded in a bell-clear tone, pushing for all she was worth against the rungs of the high chair.

"She can talk already?" Briony stared in awe at the chubby little miracle before her. "Isn't she smart."

"I think she's a genius, but then again, I may be biased." Tyrel laughed as he wiped the sticky crumbs off Cristine's fingers, then unfastened her from the high chair. He held her out to Briony. "Actually, she favors three words at the moment. *No, up* and *Nan.* Not a lot, but they're effective."

Briony awkwardly cuddled the little girl to her body, her hands fumbling as they sought a secure hold. No matter how much she'd dreamed of holding Bridget's child, she obviously wasn't any good at this!

"Nan?" she asked, glancing up at Tyrel for a second.

"My mother. She's been helping me out with Cris since Andrea died." He adjusted Cristine on her lap, grinning at her look of panic. "It's intimidating at first, but you'll get the hang of it soon enough."

Briony doubted that. It felt as if she were holding an eel. The soft downy skin was so silky smooth, it was almost slippery, and that was complicated by Cristine's churning legs and waving arms.

"Does she always wiggle like this?" Bri asked, biting her bottom lip as she fought to hold on while the baby bounced up and down.

"The only time Cristine stops moving is when she's asleep," a proud voice from the doorway informed them. A tiny woman with gray-streaked hair and crutches under both arms hobbled into the room.

"I'm Monica Demens, Ty's mother." She made a face. "I'd shake your hand but I'm not sure I can do it without falling down."

"You're supposed to be sitting down, Mother." Ty pushed a chair forward, then held out one hand. "Come on. The doctor said to keep that leg up as often as possible."

Mrs. Demens eased herself into the chair, then tilted her head back and glowered at her son. "It isn't possible to keep my leg up and move around,'' she told him grumpily.

Briony hid her smile as Tyrel sighed. He took the crutches and placed them out of the way behind a door.

''So don't move around,'' he advised laconically.

Monica ignored him, her eyes moving from Briony to the baby and back again. She peered up at Ty, obviously awaiting an introduction.

''This is Miss Green. She believes she's Cristine's aunt. She has an adoption paper signed by Andrea to prove it.''

''But I thought that you didn't know…''

Briony watched the silent interplay between mother and son. Whatever message Tyrel telegraphed his mother, she seemed to understand. She nodded once, took a deep breath, then turned her attention on Briony.

''Have you come to take Cristine?'' she demanded frankly.

Briony blinked in confusion.

''Come to— *Me?*'' She shook her head vehemently. ''No!''

The idea was so ludicrous it was laughable. Her? Look after a baby?

''Good gracious, no!'' She gulped down the unexpected rush of emotion. ''No, I'd never dream of doing that.''

Relief washed over their faces, almost lifting the dark cloud of fear from Tyrel's eyes. Why *was* he so afraid?

''My sister wanted her baby to live here, and I would never go against her wishes.'' Bri explained again about her sister's death and the diary.

''I'm starting a new job in a month, you see,'' she

added when Mrs. Demens frowned. "I just finished
my studies and I thought I'd use the next few weeks
to make sure little Cristine here was well cared for.
Once I get back into the lab, I forget everything."

"Lab?" Mrs. Demens's eyebrows rose enquiringly.

"I'm a research scientist—a botanist. I've just taken
a job in Calgary." She smiled up at Tyrel. "Actually,
my first assignment is some work for the park service.
They want to introduce a disease-resistant spruce
tree." She shifted Cristine just a little, gaining confidence the longer she held the wriggling bundle of energy.

"I've heard some talk about that." Tyrel watched
her closely, his words guarded.

Bri understood his reserve. The park service preferred its ideas to be kept under wraps until fully developed. She was used to the solitary nature of the
work. It wouldn't be a hardship not to discuss it. After
all, she mused with a sadness that wouldn't be silenced, who would she discuss it with? She didn't have
anyone in her life anymore.

"It's rather intense work. I don't expect to have
much freedom once I start, so now seemed the best
time to visit. I hope that's not a problem." Would he
understand that she had to be certain Bridget's daughter was all right?

"No, not a problem at all."

Tyrel shook his dark head once, his words stilted
but polite. He turned away and began loading the
dishes into the dishwasher.

"I'm afraid I know less than nothing about babies."
She volunteered the information frankly. There was no
point trying to hide it. "Bridget and I were the only
two in our family."

"Was she older than you?" Mrs. Demens obediently laid her leg across the chair her son had placed nearby, her fingers rubbing her knee. "You seem so young to be a scientist."

"Everyone says that." Briony laughed. "Actually, we were the same age. We were twins. Just not identical." She glanced down at the shiny head tucked beneath her chin.

"I'm not sure I was as good a sister as I should have been," she murmured softly, staring at the features so like her sister's. "Bridget was—a free spirit, I guess you'd say. She had to experiment, find her niche. I always loved nature. I knew pretty early on that was my direction."

Mrs. Demens reached out and patted her hand.

"I understand, dear. Children are often quite different from their siblings, twins or not. Ty is bossy and a tyrant," she teased, with a smile in her son's direction, "but he'll fight you for his forest. It's like his best friend. His brother got hooked on engines and never looked back. My daughter doesn't resemble either of them, thank goodness."

"No, Giselle's a perfectionist who thinks she knows everything." Tyrel's dry voice broke into their conversation. "Which is why I want you to get to her house and take a vacation before she decides to pay me a visit. Can you imagine how she'd view this kitchen?" He rolled his eyes. "She'd close me down."

"Don't start that again. I can't possibly leave you with no one to care for Cristine." Mrs. Demens fidgeted nervously. "We've explored all the options, Ty. There isn't any other way unless you're willing to let the child go. Don't worry, I'll manage with this ankle."

Briony frowned. Let Cristine go? What did that mean?

"No, you won't 'manage,'" he said, his voice hard and cool. "I'll find another solution. There's no way I'm letting anyone else raise my daughter. It's my one chance to be a father, and I'm not handing that off to anyone."

His "one chance"? What a strange thing to say. Had he loved his wife that much? Bri couldn't figure it all out, but she could see his face tighten up into a mask that hinted anger as he bit off the words.

"But Ty—"

"No, Mom. You know how I feel about Cristine staying here, in her own home. I don't want to shuffle her around from one caregiver to another."

Bri watched him study his mother's anxious face. Her skin prickled when his brown eyes softened, the glow of love darkening them to a rich chocolate that melted his mother's worry. He reached out a hand and touched her shoulder.

How would it feel to be loved like that?

"You've done more than enough, Mom. If you weren't already worn to a frazzle, you would never have hurt yourself."

"Such a silly accident." Mrs. Demens clucked her disgust. "Surely I'm not so old and tired that I must trip over every single toy the child drops."

"You wouldn't be so tired if you'd go to Giselle's and rest for a while. As I've asked." His voice held a hint of teasing.

Briony politely tried to pretend she couldn't hear a word of their conversation. But it wasn't easy, sitting there in the middle of the kitchen, smack-dab between the man and his mother. It was obvious that Tyrel wanted his mother to go, and equally obvious that the older woman felt she couldn't. Still, it was none of Bri's business.

Briony concentrated on Cristine, bouncing her gently on her knee. When a burst of giggles erupted, she tried it again, pleased at this small success.

"You're good at that. She loves movement of any kind." Tyrel stood beside her, watching his daughter reach for the gold chain around Bri's neck. "But don't let her get hold of that. She'll either try to eat it or wreck it completely."

"Oh." Bri tucked her necklace safely under her shirt collar. "It's rather special. Bridget gave it to me when we were kids—the first piece in my antique jewelry collection. Thanks for warning me."

"Where are you staying, dear?" Mrs. Demens's gray eyes glittered with suppressed excitement. "You did say you were staying?"

"Well, I intend to see more of Banff, in preparation for my work, so I rented a room at a bed-and-breakfast," she told them, secretly hoping they wouldn't think her too forward. "I actually have a month before my job starts. I thought if everything with the baby was all right, I'd spend some time hiking the area, get a feel for the kind of reforestation the park is looking for."

Did Tyrel's hands hesitate just then? Briony wasn't sure. Perhaps he hated the idea of her butting into his family, of her just walking in and assuming they'd let her see Cristine. Mrs. Demens, at least, seemed to have no problem with her staying.

"Aha. Perhaps you wouldn't mind stopping by for the next few days, then? It would be nice to have a helper to lend a hand looking after Miss Cris," she added, one eyebrow lifting as the little girl pumped her legs with glee.

"Mother! You can't ask a perfect stranger to baby-sit my daughter!" Tyrel stared at his mother as if she'd taken leave of her senses. He pivoted on his heels, cheeks dark with embarrassment as he faced Briony.

"Don't feel obligated to agree to anything Mother says, Miss Green. Though, you're more than welcome to visit Cristine whenever you like. It seems she's taken a liking to you."

His eyes glowed with fatherly pride. They all watched his daughter brush her baby fingers reverently over Briony's bright hair. For once she was glad she'd left it loose.

"She's so precious," Briony whispered. A thrill of pure delight trickled through her body when the baby fingers cupped against her cheek.

She wanted to stay, to watch Cristine, to store away the memories of babyhood that she would never share with a child of her own. In a flash of longing she made the decision.

"If you're sure you don't mind, I would like to see her again. I'd be happy to help out however I could. I've been told I'm quite good at organizing."

Tyrel froze, his eyes unfathomable as they studied her. Time dragged.

He questions my motives.

She should have seen that earlier, should have shown him the documents before now. One glance at Tyrel Demens with his daughter was enough to prove that he wouldn't willingly allow a total stranger to care for his beloved child without some assurance.

Bri shifted the baby's weight into one arm, hung on tightly, then reached down for her purse.

"I thought you'd probably want references for me to see her," she explained, holding out a sheaf of papers. "These are from my parents' lawyer. He handled their estate last year. I've known him for twenty years. This is from the professor who recommended me for the job at Bio-Tek."

She sat silently as he carefully read through each one.

"If you need more, I have a friend who works with the Royal Canadian Mounted Police in Calgary. You could phone him." She waited, breathless until he finally nodded.

"No, this is fine." He glanced at his mother, then back at Briony. A tired sigh reverberated through his chest. "All right, we'd be glad to have you. But don't let Mother bully you. She likes to have her own way."

Once more Briony witnessed the glow of love in the glance he bestowed on his mother. She felt warmed by it, thrilled that Cristine would know that same love in her own life. Bridget had chosen these people very well.

"Tyrel! I don't bully. I merely suggest." Mrs. Demens worked hard to hide the note of weariness in her voice, but her pinched cheeks and wince of pain when she shifted in her chair gave her away.

"Go and lie down, Mother. I'll take care of Cristine. You need to get your bearings back after that fall." He helped her stand, watched as she moved her crutches into place.

"You've taken too much time off as it is, Ty. You should be at work, not babying me." She reached out to brush a hand over the baby's hair. "You sweet thing," she whispered. Her eyes shifted, met Bri's.

"It was a pleasure to meet you, Briony Green. I'll

look forward to seeing you tomorrow. Is seven-thirty too early for you to visit your niece?''

"Mother!''

"Of course it's not too early. I'm always up with the birds.'' Briony ignored Tyrel's loud protest and smiled her acceptance. "I hope you have a good rest, Mrs. Demens.''

"I knew God would work this out,'' Mrs. Demens mumbled as she hobbled over the dirty floor and around the corner. Her voice whispered back. "It just takes a little faith.''

Tyrel waited until his mother was well out of earshot, then he snorted his disgust. "It takes nerve, she means.'' He shook his head at Briony. "I'm sorry about that. It's presumptuous of her to assume you can just drop everything to help us out.''

Bri smiled down at the baby in her lap who was studying them with her huge blue eyes.

"I came to Banff to meet my niece, Mr. Demens,'' she said quietly. "If I can help out in any way, I'm very pleased to do so. After all you've done for Bridget's daughter, I think a few hours lending a hand with her care is the very least I can offer. It can't be that difficult to care for a child.''

Cristine galloped her agreement, her legs churning with excitement as she waved madly.

But Tyrel clearly was not thrilled by the prospect of Briony's arrival in his household. He looked grim, out of sorts.

"I still don't understand all of this adoption business,'' he muttered. "My wife handled most of the details, so I wasn't involved with every step of the process. But I do know what she told me. Surely there would have been some papers, something she'd have shown me or told me about if she'd known the birth mother." His forehead pleated in a frown of concentration.

"You knew nothing about Bridget?" Briony's heart ached for his pain. How hard it must be to raise a child, even a beloved one, on your own.

"No, nothing," he murmured. His long black lashes drooped closed as he thought it through. "I asked about the mother several times, in case of a medical emergency or something. The lawyer mailed us a medical record, but that's all. My wife said he insisted the mother was adamant that we not know her name." His eyes pierced Briony with their questions.

"But my sister specifically left this certificate so I'd know about the adoption. And she certainly knew your wife," she murmured.

"No, my wife never met the baby's mother," he contradicted her.

"Perhaps you feel that I'm lying, that Cristine isn't my niece?" Briony tried to keep the frustration out of her voice. Why was he making this so hard?

"I have some of Bridget's baby pictures. If you saw them and compared them to Cristine, you'd see the similarity."

"I can see it just by looking at you. You have the same eyes, the same hair, even the same little cleft in your chin." A wry grin twisted his smile. "It's obvious that you are related to her. I have no valid reason to doubt your paper or your word. It's just...odd."

"I suppose it seems that way," she agreed quietly. "I can only tell you that Bridget knew you by name, both of you. I haven't read her whole diary, just the first few pages where she talks about coming to Banff, getting a job, her pregnancy. I skimmed parts, but it

seems obvious that she was determined her child have
parents she'd handpicked. You and your wife obviously met her specifications.''

He digested that for a moment, then sank down onto
the chair across from her, long khaki-covered legs
splayed out in front.

''She names *me?*'' The caustic words hissed out between his teeth, as if he could hardly bear to say them.

''No.'' Briony shook her head. She held Cristine
under her arms, letting her legs dangle between her
knees as she spoke. It was easier if she didn't look at
him, didn't see the confusion and pain in his eyes. ''I
haven't seen your name in there yet. Just your wife's.
'Andrea's husband is a forest ranger. They seem like
good people' is what it said.''

''I see.'' He tented his fingers and studied the con-
figuration for several moments. Then his head lifted,
those glowing brown eyes searching hers.

''I'd like to read her exact words for myself,'' he
said in clear and crisp tones that brooked no nonsense.
''I'd like to know exactly what she said about us. In
fact, I'd like to keep that diary for Cristine, to give her
when she grows up.''

Briony gulped. She hadn't expected this, though she
probably should have.

''I haven't read it all myself yet. I, uh, was hoping
to get through it while I was here, to understand why
she didn't come home, why she didn't ask us for
help.'' She couldn't let go of it, not yet. It was her last
tangible link with the sister she'd never understood.

''You make it sound like there's a lot to read.'' He
watched her follow Cristine as she took several steps
across the room to rescue a plush toy behind the door.
''Surely a diary isn't that long?''

"This one is. Bridget poured her heart and soul into that book. I don't want to just casually flick through it. I want to examine everything she wrote down."

I have to understand how my sister could have given away her own child, the one thing I will never have.

"Yes, of course." His face softened as he took Cristine onto his lap, the bunny firmly clasped against her chest. "Believe me, I know exactly how hard it is to lose someone." His voice changed, hardened. "It's just that I'd like to make sure that Cristine has all the information there is about her birth mother." His eyes glittered with fierce possession as his hands closed protectively around the energetic little body. "I don't want her to be hurt by the past. I won't allow that."

"No. Of course you won't."

The love flooded into his face once more as he cradled the baby in his arms, swinging her back and forth as she giggled her glee. What an abundance of love he had to shower on this precious little girl.

How she envied him that.

Tyrel glanced up at Briony, his eyes intent on her face. "It's her father I'm thinking about, too," he murmured, a roughness catching at his low voice. "What if he comes back, makes some prior claim?"

It was clear to Briony that the very idea only added to his misery. She shrugged helplessly. Tyrel's worry and concern for his daughter were painfully obvious, even though she'd only known him for mere minutes. She owed it to her niece and to him to find out all of the truth, to leave knowing nothing could separate them.

"I don't know about the father," she murmured, gathering her purse into her hand as she stood. "But

I promise I'll read more tonight, try and figure it all out. I'll let you know what I find.''

Tyrel rocked to his feet in one lithe roll and followed Briony to the door, Cristine perched high against his broad chest. He stood there for a moment, one big palm over the doorknob.

"May I ask you something?" He didn't look at her.

"Sure." Briony stood still, hands squeezed tight against the leather of her bag, hoping he wouldn't ask her to not come back.

She couldn't explain it to him, couldn't define the reason she felt drawn to this house, couldn't rationalize how her cool-headed scientist heart was inexplicably lured to the fragile child he held.

How her colleagues would laugh. Dr. Briony Green with emotions? No one would believe it. But that's the way she wanted it.

"Go ahead. Ask me whatever you'd like."

"Why didn't you read the diary through before you came? Why read only enough to learn about Cristine?" He blurted out the words in a rush of controlled agitation. "Why not learn all you could before you drove here?"

"I suppose it must seem odd to just walk into your lives." How could she expect him to understand? The need to see this precious baby had gripped her heart the day she'd found her sister's letter. Briony tried again.

"It's just that—" She stopped, lifted her head and looked him directly in the eye. "Bridget was never particularly spiritual. She scorned most things about God when we were teenagers. But before she died, she told me she'd found God here. That she came to understand His love when she lived in Banff."

He nodded slowly.

"You wanted to be in this special place when you learned what changed her." He smiled, his face soft, understanding. "Of course. I'm sorry I probed. It must be hard for you to understand how God could have let something like this happen. I know I've often asked myself the same thing."

Briony blinked away the tears, her eyes widening in surprise.

"Oh, no, I've never wondered that at all." His frown surprised her. "I know that God has everything in His hands. If He allowed it, it's because it's for the best." She brushed a hand down Cristine's bare leg.

"Then, why—"

"Why do I want to read her diary here?" She smiled at him. "It's really quite a selfish reason. I want to read it in the place where she finally came to feel His tender touch. I want to read how He softened her aching heart and molded it to His will."

Briony pretended to move a wisp of hair out of the way, but in truth she needed a moment to organize her words.

"Once I know, then I want to praise Him for doing all that for my sister, a child He loved enough to let stray from Him, and then lead back to His heart." She tugged open the door and stepped across the threshold.

"I guess I want to see His love at work in Bridget's words," she confessed in a sudden rush. "Goodbye."

Before he could laugh at her foolishness, Briony pulled the door closed and hurried over to her car.

But later that evening as she sat in her bedroom and stared at the thick leather cover of her sister's diary, she wondered if coming here had been the right thing to do.

"How could he not have known about Bridget?" she asked aloud. "Didn't he care enough to be involved?"

But that didn't make sense. For whatever Tyrel Demens was, he had clearly demonstrated that he went out of his way to love, protect and care for his family. In every way that counted, Tyrel was Cristine's daddy.

"Something about this whole situation just isn't right," she confided to the Father. "I just hope that I don't make it worse."

Chapter Two

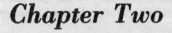

D-d-ding, dong.

Ty lifted one sleep-glazed eyelid and peered at the clock. Seven-fifteen. Couldn't be the alarm. Anyway, he hadn't set it.

The noise intruded again.

Ah, the doorbell.

He squeezed his gritty eyes closed and tried to remember if someone was supposed to ring his doorbell at this hour of the morning. He couldn't think of a single soul.

When the noise bonged through the house for the third time, Ty lurched out of bed, grabbed a robe and flew down the stairs, tying the sash around his waist as he went.

"Please stay asleep, Cristine," he begged in a whisper. That plea turned into a yowl when he stubbed his toe on the sofa. Ty quashed a second howl of pain as he passed through the living room, temper inching upward as the doorbell pealed again.

"What?" He yanked the door open and glared.

"Good morning. I was beginning to wonder if I was too early."

Ty took a cool refreshing breath of the dew-laden air and frowned. It looked like Miss Mary Sunshine had come to visit.

Dr. Briony Green stood on his doorstep, face freshly scrubbed, long blond hair flowing loose and shining down her back, her navy jeans and jacket clean and pressed. In one hand she clutched a battered briefcase that bulged.

Her face beamed a happy smile at him as she saluted. "Ready, willing and reporting for duty, sir." Briony singsonged the words as she clicked her heels together.

Ty blinked, the events of the night before tumbling in a cloudy mixture through his brain. She *was* supposed to be here, he thought vaguely, though he couldn't remember exactly why. So much had happened since he'd last seen her.

He was without a baby-sitter for Cristine. That thought reigned paramount in the confused babble of his brain. Ty rubbed his sore toe and sighed. He wasn't up to entertaining.

Still, he couldn't just leave her standing there.

"Oh. Yeah. Sure. Uh, come on in." He held the door open even as he wondered how fast he could get rid of her. He needed—no, craved sleep. Mind-numbing, body-refreshing sleep.

Briony took a careful look around, nodded.

"If you're sure. It looks like no one's up yet. I thought your mother said everything would be clicking by now." She stepped through the door, closed it and peered up at him. "You look awful."

"That's nice to know," he mumbled, rasping a hand

against his jaw. "Thank you very much for sharing."
He waved a hand around the room. "Help yourself to
whatever you need. I'll go have a shower. Then I've
got to start hunting for a sitter."

He'd almost made it out of the kitchen before his
little gray cells rearranged themselves.

Wait a minute! Baby-sitter? That was her, wasn't it?

He pivoted, bare feet squeaking on the linoleum, and
stared at her, wondering if he dared ask her to help.
Just for a day. Or two.

"Was it a rough night?" Briony set her handbag
down on the only bit of counter still visible, then
tucked her briefcase under a chair, bottom lip caught
between her teeth.

Ty grinned. Her expression didn't require transla-
tion. The good doctor preferred the sterile conditions
of a laboratory. His kitchen did not pass the test.

Ty needed a few minutes to get everything func-
tioning. Just a little bit of time to decide whether he
dared trust her with his most precious possession. He
raked a hand through his hair, mentally assessing
Briony Green.

She stood silent under his study, feet together, hands
folded in front of her, eyes quirked in a semi-frown as
she studied the remains of his last meal with distaste.

She was smart, she was educated, she wasn't dis-
abled with crutches and she'd already met Cristine.
But most of all, she was here, ready, willing and able
to pitch in for one solid month.

Ty sighed. The sum total of his scrutiny was a definite "yes." It might not be the holiday of her dreams,
but she *had* wanted to see her niece. It was too good
to turn down.

"I've had a horrible night," he told her solemnly.

"I'll tell you about it as soon as I get that shower, okay? Maybe hot water will wake me up." He waited for her assent. "Cristine's not awake yet so we might get a moment to talk."

He knew it was underhanded, tantalizing her with the baby like that. But he was desperate. He breathed again when she nodded.

"Go ahead and shower. Take your time." Her big blue eyes glowed with sympathy. "I'll listen for her." She glanced around, nose wrinkling at the messy room. "In the meantime, I believe I'll just straighten up a bit."

"Bless you." Ty sighed with heartfelt thanksgiving. He headed for the stairs before she could change her mind. "If you could put on a pot of coffee, that would be wonderful. The grounds are in the fridge."

With superhuman strength, Ty forced himself to ignore the beckoning warmth of his king-size bed and walk straight past it to the shower. Ten minutes later, shaved, bathed and optimistically dressed in his uniform, he was wide awake and almost ready to plead for heavenly help as he started downstairs, glad that, for once, Cris had missed her usual six a.m. wake-up call.

On the main floor of his home, all traces of the night's activities had been erased. The furniture sat fluffed and prim, the tables polished, the lamps straight, and the blinds open to the morning sun. The kitchen looked just as neat, though an odd smell permeated the room.

"Ah, coffee," he sighed, spotting the full carafe. "That's exactly what I need. Thanks so much for helping out, Briony."

Ty grabbed a mug and poured himself a huge

amount of the potent black brew. He noticed Briony frowning at him, and lifted his mug in acknowledgment.

"I don't usually drink this much coffee," he told her with a grin. "But I need it today."

"I'm not sure it's..."

Her voice died away as he took a swig. She stood, fingers knotted together, studying his face with a worried frown as he tasted the bitter burnt liquid.

There was nothing Ty wanted more just then than to spit the horrible acrid stuff into the sink and wash out his mouth with antiseptic. In all his years with the other park wardens, he had never tasted anything quite so awful as her coffee!

"Oh, my—" He swallowed his words, refused to gag.

Briony had come to his assistance today, and he desperately needed her help. He wouldn't offend her—not for the sake of coffee.

"It's very...unusual," he told her, setting his mug on the counter. "Thanks for doing that." He grabbed a chair and sat down, throat still burning with the awful taste.

"It's bad, isn't it." She sighed, her big eyes, so like his daughter's, brimming with apology. "I didn't think it smelled right, but I wanted to at least try. Usually I'm quite good with measurements, but I couldn't find the directions anywhere."

"How much coffee did you use?" he asked carefully, praying he wouldn't offend her.

"Just half a cup." Her eyes blinked innocence.

Half a cup of grounds? Ty swallowed, no longer surprised at the darkness or the bitter aftertaste.

She was speaking again, blue eyes pensive as she

methodically sorted through the process. "The numbers are worn off the carafe, and I wasn't sure exactly how much it made, so I thought it must be about the same as the one in the lab at the university."

"Ah." That explained it. Coffee from a lab. Some scientific experiment, no doubt. "Your pot was probably larger," he offered.

"Do you think so?" She considered that for a moment. "Perhaps that's it. Though, to tell you the truth, I haven't made coffee for a long time." She frowned, her forefinger tapping against her chin. "The other students seemed to prefer making it themselves. Mine never tasted quite the same as theirs, though I tried all their secret tricks."

"Secret tricks," he repeated stupidly, stunned by her beauty. The sunshine poured in, turning her hair to a golden halo. He shook his head, focused on the present. "What secret tricks are there to making coffee?"

"Well, I added the salt. One teaspoon for a full pot, they used to say. Your pot does look a little smaller." She peered at the glass carafe. "Perhaps it should have been less."

"Salt." He nodded, rolling his tongue around in his mouth. What in the world was salt doing in his coffee?

"Yes. It's supposed to keep the scale off or something." Briony shrugged. "I can't remember the reason, but it sort of made sense. And a pinch of pepper, too. To enhance the flavor, I think. I forget what pepper does." Eyes downcast, she played with a ringlet that drooped over one ear.

"Actually, it might have been more than a pinch," she admitted, lifting her eyes to meet his and giving an apologetic smile. "The lid came off."

"Uh-huh." Pepper? Now Ty knew why his throat burned. He coughed discreetly behind his hand, trying to hide a smile at the ridiculousness of adding pepper to coffee. Surely these "friends" must have been fooling her!

"I take it you don't drink coffee."

"Oh, I love a good cup of coffee." Her eyes opened wide. "I just can't seem to make one. I usually buy instant," she told him cheerfully. "And I never put salt or pepper in it. I think it tastes funny." Her nose scrunched up at the remembered smell.

Ty choked back a laugh and mentally made a note to purchase a new coffeemaker. That pepper would be a long time dripping through.

"Do you want me to try again?" she asked, head tilted to one side, eyes glazing over as she delved into some mental calculations. "Maybe if I used twenty percent more grounds—"

"Never mind," he said hastily. "I don't really have time, anyway."

"Did something happen last night?" Briony's voice was quiet, hesitant. As if she were worried he'd boot her out for snooping.

If she only knew!

"My mother fell again last night." As he sank into a chair, his mind relived that awful *clunk.*

"Oh, no!" Briony clapped a hand over her mouth. "Was she badly hurt?"

"Well, she didn't help anything." It hurt to say it, pained him even more to know it was all his fault. "Cristine cried out in her sleep. I didn't hear her right away. By the time I did, Mother was already going to her. She stumbled over something and fell."

"How awful! I'm really sorry." Briony reached out

a hand to touch his arm. "I suppose she's in the hospital now?"

He shook his head. "She's at my sister's. In Calgary. After they fixed her up, I drove her there. Giselle's guest bedroom is on the main floor. Mom will be able to rest there. Finally."

"Calgary?" She stared. "But that's over three hours of driving! Not to mention how long it took to x-ray and treat her."

He nodded, one hand massaging the back of his neck. "Believe me, I know exactly how long it took. I got to bed about four-thirty. I would have stayed but my sister had company—her son's teenage friends took over the basement."

"I'm very sorry."

It was just a whisper, but Ty could hear the heartfelt meaning in her words.

"I am, too. Though I've been trying to get my mother to take a break for months now, I would have preferred she didn't take it in the leg."

Briony's solemn look didn't alter.

Ty sighed. "That was a joke."

She didn't even crack a smile. One finger tapped against her chin as she stared at the jam-spattered cabinet door. "It leaves you in the lurch, though. Doesn't it?" She fiddled with the crease in her jeans now, obviously deep in thought. "You'll need to find someone to watch your daughter."

Something inside Ty gave a twist of relief at her words. "His daughter," she'd said. She obviously didn't think of Cris as anything else. That was reassuring. For a while last night he'd wondered if she was seeking custody of the little girl for her own reasons.

"Yes, I'll need to find someone right away." He

took a deep breath and plunged in. "I was hoping maybe you could help."

"Me?"

Briony gawked at him, her blue eyes expanding into huge sapphire pools that reminded him of the untouched mountain lakes tucked away in Banff's remote valleys.

She swallowed, her long, pale throat clearly defined in the opening of her shirt. Her shoulders went back.

"Of course, I'll help all I can." The little wobble in her voice quickly disappeared. "I told your mother that last night. But I don't know anything about child care. I'm afraid I wouldn't know where to begin."

Ty empathized with the helplessness flooding her face. He'd felt the same way when Cristine had come into their lives, even more so after God had taken Andrea. That was when he'd realized he was responsible for a tiny helpless baby.

He reached out and touched Briony's delicate hand, stilling its fluttering motions with a squeeze. A tingle of electricity shot through him. Her silky smooth skin radiated a warmth he saw reflected in her eyes.

"It's not really that hard, though it takes a lot of energy." How strange that she should affect him like this—make him nervous and unsure of himself. He was never unsure. Ty tried to sound confident. "You just have to meet her needs."

Briony's glance flew from his hand on hers to his face. "But I have no idea what those needs are." She sounded as if children were from another world.

Ty grinned. Perhaps in her lab they were. Just the thought of Cristine in a pristine sterile environment for more than ten seconds tickled his funny bone.

"Pretty basic needs at her age," he answered.

"Clean, dry and fed. A hug now and then. Protection from dangerous situations. Didn't you ever baby-sit?" He studied her curiously.

"No. Never."

That was all. No explanation, no reason. He sensed there was something behind that, but now wasn't the time to question her.

The telephone rang, breaking the silence.

Ty answered and listened, his heart sinking at the news. "I'll be there as soon as I can," he told his boss. "I'm just not sure when that will be." He sighed as he listened to the lecture on his multiple absences over the past few months.

The reminder chewed at his pride.

"I know I've asked for a lot of time off, John. But my daughter comes first. Always." A few more directions, a plea to handle it, and Ty hung up the phone.

"More problems." Briony sat primly in her chair, waiting. She was not asking a question.

Ty nodded. "A child is missing. She wandered away from her campsite early this morning." He wondered if he should tell all of it, then decided it couldn't hurt. No doubt Briony already knew all about his job. "I'm supposed to lead a search party."

"But you don't want to leave Cristine." She kept her eyes on her hands. "Especially not with someone like me who doesn't know the first thing about parenting. I understand."

She'd refused before he could even ask. Ty turned away to pick up the phone book, shoulders slumping in defeat.

"It's all right. I'll find someone to look after her. The kids are still in school, of course, but maybe..." He bent over the pages, his mind busy.

He dialed a number and explained his problem. Then did it again. And again. By the sixth time, frustration held him tight in its grip.

"I'm sorry, Ty, but I just can't. Herb's away and the twins have chicken pox. I wouldn't dream of exposing Cristine to that." Mary MacGregor apologized profusely. "I'm sorry I can't be more help. It's made things really difficult with that flu that's going around. They even had to close the day-care center."

Ty's heart dropped to his shoes as he thanked his talkative neighbor, then hung up. The day-care center had been his last hope.

"Oh, boy, am I ever in trouble." He dropped his head into his hands, feeling as desperate as a man on death row.

"Is everything all right?"

Ty glanced up. The gorgeous scientist stood in the doorway, her arms wrapped around Cristine. Nervous expectation washed over her face as she met his stare. Ty swallowed, his heart thumping with pride as his baby played happily with Briony's necklace, cooing her pleasure as she stroked her hand over the shining sapphire that hung suspended from an antique gold chain.

"Cristine woke up a few minutes ago. I didn't want to disturb your phone call so I got her up myself." She frowned, her eyes on the puffy bottom of the fuzzy sleeper. "I'm not exactly sure I got her diaper on right. It looks a little baggy."

"It looks fine."

At the sound of his voice, Cristine turned her head toward him. Her chubby face broke out in a delighted smile as she stretched her arms toward him.

"Up!"

Ty scooped her into his arms and held her close, pressing his face into her neck. He kissed the downy skin, feeling the love surge inside him. This perfect joy made everything else bearable.

"Good morning, sweetheart. How's Daddy's girl?" He froze as her baby lips brushed against his cheek, thrilled beyond measure by that delicate touch. "I love you, sweetheart," he whispered, his throat hot and tight with emotion.

"Did you find someone?" Briony pulled the high chair close to the table, watching every move as he set the little girl in it and fastened a strap that prevented her from slipping out.

"No. There's no one." The hopelessness of it overwhelmed him as he admitted the truth. "It's my own fault. I should have hired a full-time caregiver ages ago, before I used up my sick leave and holidays."

"Oh."

What else was there for her to say? How could she possibly understand how difficult it had been?

"I've taken so many days off, asked someone else to fill in for me so often, that I'm in danger of getting laid off, instead of bucking for the promotion I wanted. And now I can't find anyone to look after Cristine."

Ty knew he should have managed better, should have conducted his affairs in a more organized fashion. Most of all, he should have found someone to replace his mother long ago. He'd depended on her for too long, and now his job was jeopardized.

"There's me."

His head jerked up at her words, his hand stilling against Cristine's soft curls.

"I know I have no credentials to offer, no experience at this at all. But if you show me the basics, I

ought to be able to handle it.'' Her shoulders thrust
back, her chin jutted out. ''I'm a competent scientist
with a PhD, Mr. Demens. Surely I ought to be able to
care for a little girl, my own niece, for a few hours.''

''It's Ty.'' He could see how much the words cost
her. Worry and fear hung like shadowy specters in the
back of her eyes, waiting to pounce at the first sign of
failure.

And she would fail. They all had. It was only natural. But Ty had a hunch Briony Green had contemplated that possibility and offered anyway. Even now
her hands shook as they smoothed Cristine's bib into
place.

''I can do this,'' she whispered, her face pale but
composed. ''I can do this. For Bridget.'' She stood,
small and defenseless before him, determination surrounding her like a cloak.

''I wouldn't dream of asking,'' he explained kindly.
''It isn't your problem. If you did stay, all you'd be
doing is prolonging my problem. You have to go to
your new job in a month, and I'd be back to square
one.''

Briony nodded thoughtfully. He could see her mind
sorting through the possibilities.

''I know it's not a full reprieve,'' she agreed at last.
''I don't have all the answers. But I know Someone
who does, and I'll be praying that He will make all
things work together.'' She smiled. ''In the meantime,
if you can bear to allow me to care for your daughter,
I promise you I'll give her all my attention.''

''You're sure?'' Did he dare take her up on it? Did
he dare believe that God had answered the last prayer
he'd vowed ever to pray?

''I'm positive.'' Briony stared down at Cristine,

eyes pensive. "Bridget never asked me for help while she was alive. But maybe, through her daughter, I can help her now."

Ty studied her for several moments, as she turned her attention to Cris. How tenderly she spoke to the little girl, offered her a toy, smiled at her giggles of joy.

Hadn't he once believed that God cared for His children in all circumstances? Hadn't his mother told him over and over that God would answer in His own good time? Maybe, just maybe…

Ty took a deep breath. "Very well, if you're willing, thank you. I appreciate your help more than you can possibly imagine."

He launched into a description of Cristine's day, the foods she ate, the toys she loved, what she couldn't have, slowing down only when Briony missed scribbling something on her notepad and asked him to repeat.

"She's very healthy. No allergies we know of. But she does keep you moving. You can't let up your guard for a moment," he warned, setting a bowl of cereal in front of his daughter. He fed her a spoonful.

Briony studied his movements clinically, as if it were an experiment she would have to replicate in order to meet some criterion. Ty wondered for the thousandth time if he was doing the right thing, but he shoved the doubts away.

If God was who his mother said, if He truly cared about them, He'd come through. Maybe, just this once, He'd come through.

Ty concentrated on giving her his numbers. "Everything's written down on the list on the fridge. If you need me, I've got my cell phone. It generally works in the mountains, but if there's a problem, any kind of trouble, just call the park office. If I can't get here immediately, they'll send someone who can.''

"Yes. Certainly. Got that.''

Ty could see her absorbing every detail, organizing and filing each tidbit of information in precise, logical order. He tried to be patient while he waited.

The phone rang again, and he answered.

"They've found some bear tracks in the area," he told Briony after he hung up several moments later. "I have to report in now." He studied her pale face. "Are you sure you can do this?"

"Maybe not exactly the way you've been doing it," she quipped, her voice shaky. "But I think Cristine and I will manage. You go ahead." As if to prove she was capable, she took his place beside the high chair and began spooning the cereal into Cristine's rosebud mouth.

"She sometimes—" Ty swallowed the words as his daughter puffed out her cheeks and blew her oatmeal all over her new caregiver.

"Yes?" Briony peered up at him through the milky-white goop running through her lashes. With pinched fingers she removed three globs from her shirt and laid them on a napkin she'd carefully placed nearby.

Ty shook his head. Sometimes experience was the best teacher. "Never mind. With kids there are some things you just have to encounter firsthand." Ty snatched up two bananas, his knapsack and his jacket. He leaned down to press a kiss against Cristine's head, skillfully avoiding her dirty hands.

"Bye, darling. Be a good girl for Auntie Briony." He walked to the door, took one last look around, then met Briony's bright gaze.

"If there's anything…" he repeated.

"…I'll call you," she promised. "Don't worry. We have God on our side."

Ty headed out the door to his Jeep, wondering as he went how he was supposed to *not* worry. That was his daughter back there. His one and only child. A gift more precious than life.

"I know we haven't exactly seen eye-to-eye on things," he murmured as he steered through town to the checkpoint he'd been directed to. "I can't figure out why You do things and I don't like not knowing, or not being in control. But could you please send an angel to watch out for my little girl?"

He spared a thought for the small blond woman who had no idea what she'd gotten herself into.

"Maybe You'd better send one for Briony Green, too," he added, pulling in to the site now teeming with people. "She's kind and generous and smart, but I'm pretty sure she had no intention of spending her holiday looking after her sister's child."

Briony's words about Bridget and Andrea returned to haunt him. Andrea's signature under Bridget's on that adoption order burned into his brain. How could he not have known such a vital piece of information? Had Andrea hidden a friendship with Bridget?

"But why?" he asked himself. "Why? I was her husband. I wanted the child as much as she did."

The questions had to be stored away. For now.

But Ty knew he would find the answers. He had to.

Chapter Three

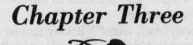

Five-and-a-half long hours later, Briony clutched the phone to her ear like a lifeline.

"Please, Clarissa, help me! I can't seem to stop her from crying." She felt the tears wet on her own cheeks and sniffed in misery. "I know she's tired, because she almost nods off. Then her little head jerks back and she starts all over again. You've got to think of something else to try."

Bri waited desperately for her friend's suggestion, never more conscious of her own helplessness than at this moment.

"Wait a minute, Bri. Blair just arrived. Maybe she's got some suggestions." A murmured conference in the background waffled over the telephone, then Clarissa returned. "I don't really know what else to tell you, honey. I've used up all my best baby-quieters. Hang on."

Bri stared at the beet-red face that glared furiously at her. About two more minutes of this and she intended to call Tyrel Demens back home permanently—bear and lost child notwithstanding. At this point she'd even *pay* for him to stay here.

Motherhood was not her forte. Hadn't she learned that lesson years ago?

"Bri?" Blair's pure clear voice sounded in her ear. "Clarissa tells me you're having some baby-sitting problems. I can't wait to hear how this came about. You, the woman who intended to devote her life to science? Baby-sitting?"

"Not now, okay, Blair?" Briony moved the phone a little nearer to Cristine's screaming mouth. Her old college buddy laughed, then surrendered.

"Okay, Bri. I get the message. Listen, does she have a stroller?"

"I don't know." Briony cast a quick glance around the room. Something navy and white was folded behind the door. "I think so. It's all flattened out, though."

"That's to make them easier to stow in the car. Usually if you push the handles apart, the seat folds down and *presto!* a stroller. Do you want me to hang on?"

"Yes." Bri carefully set the sobbing child on the now-pristine floor and moved across to grasp the stroller in both hands. Fortunately, it snapped apart with little effort. She picked the phone back up.

"Okay. Now what?"

"If she's as mad as she sounds, she's not going to settle for a few pushes in the house. You'll have to take her for a walk. The fresh air usually knocks them out in seconds." Blair stopped, said something to Clarissa, then came back on. "Make sure the seat belt holds her in securely. You don't want her to take a tumble."

"So I just get her in it and go strolling down the

street?'' Briony cast a dubious glance at her niece's writhing body. "I don't think that's going to do it, Blair."

Blair chuckled. "Oh, you don't stroll, honey. Not at first. You walk fast, pushing her along as quickly as you can. The bouncing and changing scenery usually do the trick. Either that or a car ride."

"A car ride?"

"Uh-uh. Scratch that. You can't take her unless you have a child seat, Bri. So for now, I'd bundle her into the stroller and take a walk. Probably do you good, too."

"Silence would do me the most good," Bri mumbled glumly. Silence, or a visit with her two best friends. Why hadn't she chosen to spend the month with them, at the lake, instead of getting herself tied up with a screeching bundle of contrariness?

Bridget, that's why. Bri sighed.

"Thanks a lot, Blair. I'll have to hang up, but stay near the phone, will you? I may need more help."

"I'll be here, kid. And we'll ask the Father of us all to lend you a little support, too."

Clarissa came on the line. "Don't worry, Bri. If she's dry, full, and not pushing a fever, she's just tired out and can't relax enough to sleep."

"But she's crying so hard!"

"Kids cry. It's the only way they can tell us they need something. But crying's not fatal. Okay?"

"Okay. Bye." Briony sighed, then bent down and picked up the kicking baby. "Listen, sweetie. You and I are going to take a walk. It's nice outside and you need to have a nap. A very long nap. Okay, darling?"

It took ages to get Cristine fastened into the stroller. And even longer to find a light blanket to lay over her when she fell asleep—if she ever stopped crying, that is.

"This house needs some serious organization," she muttered, finally dragging a flannelette square from between the sofa cushions.

Bri stuffed down her urge to organize, and followed Blair's directions. She wheeled the little girl outside, closed the door behind her and quickly walked down the path that led along the river.

Several people turned to stare as Cristine's wails reverberated across the water, echoing far louder and longer than Bri considered strictly necessary.

"Please, God, make her go to sleep. Please? Or even just stop bawling. She's so tired and she wants her grandma and I don't know how to help her. Please make her stop."

It took a minute to realize that Cristine was indeed silent. Briony slowed her walk, heard a whimper and immediately resumed her pace, trying to peer around the top of the stroller to see if the child was sleeping.

Four blocks later, she decided she couldn't wait any longer. She had to know if Cristine was all right, and if that meant risking waking her, well, then, she'd do it.

But Cristine, it seemed, had no intention of waking. She lay fast asleep in her soft flannel nest, her face turned to one side in a cherubic pose that sent little thrills up and down Briony's spine. This baby was so precious.

"Thank you, Lord." With a breath of relief, she rearranged the blanket so no chilly mountain breeze could touch that delicate skin, then continued on her way, absorbing the sights and sounds as she went.

Banff in June was God's creation in all its glory.

The river tumbled past, cloudy blue-green water testament to its glacial origin. Beyond the town site, craggy, ice-covered peaks blazed white in the noonday sun, nestling the steep roofs of the alpine town in their embrace.

A little bench sat tucked behind a tree, just feet away from the water's edge. Briony sank down on it with a sigh of relief.

"You're useless," she chastised herself as the weariness stole over her. "One tiny little girl, and you're like a dishrag."

She checked to be sure Cristine was still asleep. How was such a miracle possible? Today she'd witnessed Bridget's daughter falter across a toy-strewn carpet just to be held. She'd watched that little mouth consume tiny amounts of food with relish, then come back for more. And now, that sweet soul lay resting so quietly, as if she'd never given anyone a moment's trouble.

"She's a darling, Bridget," Briony whispered as she gazed across the river at the old stone bridge. "Thank you for telling me about her. Thank you for letting me share the blessing."

A *thud* on the bench beside her made Briony start.

"You scared me half to death." Ty Demens peered at his daughter, then, seemingly satisfied that she was all right, glared at Briony. "I went home to check on you and nobody was there. I thought for sure you had to go to the hospital."

"I'm not quite that incompetent!" Briony grimaced at him, secretly relieved that she hadn't been forced to use the medical facilities. "It's such a lovely afternoon, we decided to take a walk."

"And everything is all right?" He frowned, studying her as if to find a telltale sign that she was incapable of looking after his daughter. "No problems?"

"Oh, sure. There were a few things. But we worked them through." She tossed it out airily, pretending she hadn't been scared of doing something wrong. "It takes time to learn a baby's routine."

Bri smugly repeated Clarissa's words without a single qualm, then hastily changed the subject before he could ask more.

"How did your morning go? Did you find the child?"

"Yes." He nodded, a smile tugging at the corners of his mouth. "She climbed a tree when she saw the bear, but she couldn't figure out how to get down. Smart little thing."

He leaned back against the bench and tilted his face up to the sun. "I'll miss lunch if I don't take a break now."

Lunch? Briony's stomach rumbled a loud, insistent complaint at the mention of food. She offered Ty an apologetic smile. "I guess I missed breakfast."

He studied her. "I thought you were staying at a bed-and-breakfast."

"I am. I just didn't feel like bacon and eggs this morning. Nervous, I suppose. Then Cristine and I were too busy playing for me to notice the time, until now." She blinked at her watch in surprise.

"There's a fast-food place not far away. What if I picked up a couple of burgers? We could eat our lunch here. Cristine will sleep longer, I'm sure. And I know you could use the rest."

Burgers? How long since she'd eaten red meat? Briony barely kept her lips from smacking. Burgers sounded fantastic. "That would be nice," she told him demurely.

"Okay. Be right back." Ty loped off across the park, intent on his mission to secure food.

"Your daddy is a very nice man, Cristine," she whispered, watching Ty's lean body dodge tourists as he jogged across the intersection and dashed inside the fast-food place.

He's also very good-looking.

She ignored the hint from her subconscious. She wasn't interested in a relationship. But even if she were, a man with a child certainly did not merit placement on the list. She'd learned her lesson there— learned it well. Only stupid people repeated their mistakes.

"I'm sorry, Bri, but I don't think I ever really loved you."

The remembered words stung almost as fiercely now as they had six years ago. She relived those awful minutes.

"I think I was subconsciously looking for a mother for my son. I wanted to be certain he wasn't deprived of a loving home and I thought you could help me provide that. But you're not really the mother type, are you?" Her husband-to-be had smiled, as if to soften the horrible words that dripped from his lips.

"You're too obsessed with your lab and your microscope to be the kind of mother a child needs."

She'd been stunned by the comment. How could he know her so little? Her heart fractured as he continued.

"His real mother has come back, Briony. She's the only woman I'll ever love. No one can take her place. She's agreed to marry me."

And just like that, Bri's engagement was over, the

wedding canceled, the groom gone. And with him—or rather, with his son—had gone Briony's dreams.

She'd fallen in love with that little boy, given him the secret place in her heart that poured out all the love and affection she'd never known she possessed. She'd invested herself in getting to know the six-year-old, and in doing so had come to realize she wanted to be a mother.

Worse than that, she'd begun to think of them as a family.

And then, suddenly, father and son were gone, and she wasn't part of their lives anymore. She felt the sting of it even now.

"It was a good lesson to learn," she reminded herself as she studied the sleeping baby beside her. "You can't get involved with this child. She's his. All you're doing is helping him out. When the time comes, you need to be able to walk away."

Yes, that was it. Remain unemotional. Don't get involved. Do the job, then leave.

Hadn't she accepted that God had His hand on everything in her life? He'd given her a career instead of a family. She had to accept that He always knew best.

Bri stared down at Cristine. Her throat pinched closed, her breathing stuck in her chest. One month and then she'd leave. But for now, it couldn't hurt to just look, could it?

"They weren't very busy." Ty plopped down on the seat beside her. "I hope you like chocolate milk shakes. I bought the largest."

He handed her a paper cup with a straw poking out the top, and a sack. Then he paused, holding his own. "You looked awfully pensive. Is anything wrong?"

"No, nothing." Bri offered him a weak smile. At least he'd brought her a milk shake. She didn't think she could drop her defenses enough to swallow a soft drink *and* a burger.

"Rough morning, huh?" He grinned, patted her hand, then dug into his own lunch. "I know the feeling. For the first six months of her life, I don't think I slept more than an hour at a time."

"Was she sick or something?" Bri looked up from sipping her shake. "I've heard stories about newborns that don't sleep."

Ty laughed. "Oh, this little miss slept like an angel. I'm afraid the problem was me."

"You?" She waited for his response, her gaze riveted on the family sharing a picnic on the grass just a few feet away. There was a persistent ache in her heart. Bri turned away.

"Yeah. Me." Ty unwrapped his burger, took a bite and chewed thoughtfully. "I was a nervous wreck. I had to keep checking if she was breathing, that she wasn't smothered, that she didn't need a dry diaper or fresh air. She was too warm, she was too cold." He shook his head. "It's a wonder I didn't drive everybody nuts."

"A little overpossessive, were you?" She grinned, unable to visualize this in-control man at the mercy of a tiny baby.

"A lot overpossessive." His gaze slipped far away, into the past. Some emotion—dark, brooding—slipped through his eyes until they glowed almost black.

"She was so tiny, so precious. We'd wanted to have kids for ages. Then we accepted we never would."

"I'm sorry."

In front of Bri, Tyrel's face lost the grim look and

glowed with joy. "One night I came home from work—and there she was. My very own daughter. I couldn't quite believe in that miracle. Sometimes I still can't."

Briony nodded. "I felt the same way when I found that paper." She laughed. "My sister a mother? It just didn't compute."

"And yet it does. Sort of." He studied her from beneath his lashes, hiding his expression. "From what you've said, Cristine is definitely her daughter." Just the hint of a question dangled in those words.

Bri couldn't leave him hanging. She nodded. "Yes, she's the spitting image of our baby pictures. And from what I read last night, Cristine is certainly Bridget's daughter." She took a deep breath and admitted the truth. "I read on in my sister's diary last night. The dates Bridget indicates all seem to correlate with Cristine's birthday—March first, isn't it?" She waited for his nod.

"And then there are the signatures." She almost hated to remind him of his wife's part in this.

"Yes, the signatures." He folded up the wrapper from the fries, shoved it inside the bag, then dumped it and the remains of his shake into the nearby garbage can. "I still can't understand that part. Andrea was so certain the birth mother would never allow herself to be revealed." He glanced at her. "I'm not making that up, you know."

"I know." Bri had no answer to the question in his eyes. "Maybe if you told me a bit about what was going on back then, you'd remember something that would explain it," she offered, fully aware that his past was none of her business.

He frowned.

"If you're not comfortable with that, it's all right," she reassured him hurriedly. "I understand that it's painful to dig into the past."

"It's just that it's all such a blur. We had a huge forest fire in the park last year. Everyone was working extra-long shifts with not much time for sleep or anything else." His expression turned grim. "Not enough snow and a very warm winter."

"I remember." Bri closed her eyes. "Several rangers got caught in a back draft."

He nodded. "No matter how many people they brought in, we couldn't turn the tide. Sometimes we didn't even make it home, just took a sleeping bag and sacked out for a few hours." He glanced up through his lashes. "I came home as often as I could, but with the fire threatening the town, I'm afraid I was preoccupied with work."

"Of course." Bri finished her lunch, savoring the last smooth swallow of her cool milk shake. "So your wife would have had a lot of time on her own. If she met someone, made a new friend, she may not have told you about it."

"Andrea didn't go out a lot." The words slipped out on a soft murmur, as if he felt he was maligning his wife by admitting that.

"Oh." Bri waited.

"She was nervous about tourists and the strangers that always come to town. It was worse then. It would have been…unusual for her to have made a new friend," he said after a pause.

"But not impossible?"

"No. Not impossible."

But something in his voice told her he thought it very unlikely.

"Bridget found a job working in the Banff Springs Hotel. She'd worked in Reservations before, so that wasn't unusual. She loved those fancy, historic hotels."

"When did she arrive?"

Bri frowned. "I can't really tell that, but from her diary entries, it seems as if she'd been here for a while. She writes a bit about her doctor telling her to rest. A local doctor, apparently."

"I don't know any. I haven't seen a doctor in years." He shrugged. "Andrea always insisted on seeing someone in Calgary. Sometimes my sister would coax her to stay for a day or two, but my wife never spoke of meeting anyone."

Silence hung between them, punctuated by the gurgle of the river, the conversation of passing hikers and the rumble of traffic as it crossed the bridge. In the distance, Briony could see tiny, glass-enclosed gondola cars lifting up Sulphur Mountain.

"And Cristine's father?" He seemed to ask in spite of himself. "Did you find any mention of him?"

Pity welled inside her. How difficult it must be to wonder if the child you'd come to adore would be claimed by someone else.

"I'm sorry, I don't know that. Bridget doesn't mention him at all. So far."

His head jerked in a nod of understanding. His big hands twisted and tore the paper napkin into puny shreds. "But there is hope that she might. Maybe once you've read more?"

She didn't want to dash his hopes. "Perhaps." She remembered the notations she'd read. "Bridget wrote about a support group she met with."

"Support?" He stared at her. "For what?"

"I'm not sure. Alcohol, perhaps. I don't think she was ever into drugs. Anyway, I think the group met every week. She writes of several people in the group." Briony took a deep breath. "I thought perhaps I'd go to the hotel and ask if anyone remembers her, or if the group is still going."

"It's a good idea," he agreed, but a hint of warning shaded his voice. "Just don't expect too much. The population here fluctuates with the seasons. It's quite possible that many of the people she worked with last year have moved on."

"Of course." Briony nodded, her eyes on the diminutive form now stirring in the stroller. "I think perhaps I'd better start walking again. I don't want Cristine to wake up just yet." She jiggled the stroller in hopes of calming the little girl.

"I've got to get back soon, but I'll walk a little way with you." Ty adjusted his stride to match hers as they meandered back down the river walk. "Soon these streets will be overflowing with tourists," he murmured. "July is frenetic."

She followed his glance. Three buses unloaded their passengers, each of whom scurried in a different direction. She knew what Ty was thinking: how would he ever find information about his daughter in such a quickly changing community?

Briony chanced a look at him. "Don't worry, Ty. We'll find out more about Cristine. It just takes time for God to work out all the kinks."

"You have a lot of faith in God, don't you?" He stared down at her intently.

"It's the one thing that's kept me going through some pretty tough situations."

"You sound like my mother." He stopped for several moments, saying nothing as he skipped a rock across the water. When she kept going, he caught up, then offered her a timid smile. "I wish I had faith like you two. I guess I'm just one of those people who has to see to believe."

"No, you aren't." Briony shook her head. "You don't see the air, do you? But you keep right on breathing, all the same. You don't know for sure that you'll be alive and healthy next year, but you keep on planning for the future." She grinned at him. "You have faith, Ty. Maybe it just isn't developed enough."

"Like my muscles?" He huffed out a laugh.

Briony couldn't seem to keep her eyes off him. His lopsided smile tugged at her heartstrings.

"I don't think you need to worry," she whispered, her cheeks burning with embarrassment as she stared at his brown muscular arms, bare where the short-sleeved shirt ended.

He laughed. "Thanks, I think." Then his face grew serious.

"I have tried, you know. To have faith. But nothing turns out the way I expect."

She knew he was thinking about his wife. "It isn't easy," she agreed. "But if 'faith is the evidence of things hoped for,' then you can't give up. You've got to keep trusting that someday you'll understand why."

Her steps slowed, then stopped as a small stone church came into view. "First Avenue Fellowship." The name sounded familiar. Bri's mind clicked through the information, then flew back to the diary in her room.

Ty frowned at her. "Is anything wrong? You've the strangest look on your face."

"No." Bri shook her head. She pointed. "There's the church."

"The church?" He followed her gaze, a whimsical grin crinkling his eyes. "That's nothing new. It's been there for a long time, Briony. Over a hundred years." He must have sensed her excitement. "Does it mean something to you?"

"Not a thing," she assured him, hurriedly wheeling the stroller to the intersection. She waited until the coast was clear, then scooted across, fully aware that Ty was trailing behind her.

"Then, may I ask what you're doing?"

"Bridget mentioned that church in her diary. I didn't make the connection right away. I thought she was talking about a fellowship group that met someplace on First Avenue."

Bri marched up the sidewalk and stood staring at the huge sign beside the front door.

"You think this is where she came?" he asked as he ambled up beside her. All at once a sudden crush of people flowed out from the side door, and his arm curved over her back to shield Bri.

Bri's breath forgot to move. Jolts of electricity radiated from his hand to her body. Power and steely strength emanated from that touch. What was it about Ty Demens that affected her so much?

Bri took a calming breath. "I don't know if this is the place. But I think I'm going to find out." She pointed to the sign. "Look. 'Fellowship meetings every Tuesday afternoon for those who need a friend,'" she read out loud.

He looked unconvinced by her find. "But how would that connect Bridget with Andrea? We never attended this church."

"I don't know how. Yet." Bri tugged open the side door and wheeled the stroller inside. "But maybe we can find out."

They followed the long narrow hall back to a room that was obviously behind the sanctuary. A man stood rinsing out cups in a small kitchen to the left.

"Oh, hello." He smiled, his eyes moving from them to Cristine. "A bit of rest for everyone, is it?" He winked. "I'm sorry, but the meeting is over for today."

"That's all right. We didn't come for the meeting." Ty cast a dubious look around the room. "Is it for AA or something?"

The man in the kitchen shrugged, wiped his hands on the towel, then moved toward them. "Something like that. Really, I suppose it's a support group for anyone who needs a hand up."

Bri waited for Ty to ask the obvious question. But when he remained in front of a cork board, staring at the small felt handprints that decorated it, she took the bull by the horns.

"Do you ever have any expectant mothers come?" she asked in a rush. "Unwed mothers?" It seemed shameful to call Bridget by that horrid demeaning title, and yet, wasn't that exactly what she'd been?

"Sometimes we do." The man frowned. "Is there something in particular you'd like to know, Mrs...."

"Oh, sorry." Bri grinned at him. "My name is Briony Green. This is Tyrel Demens. He's a park ranger, and I'm the sitter for his daughter."

"I see. I'm Tom Winter. I'm the minister here." He shook hands with them both, then motioned toward the chairs. He waited until they'd seated themselves, his open gaze moving from one to the other. "How can I help you?"

When it became obvious that Ty had no intention of speaking, Bri took a deep breath and related their story, without going into details.

"So you see," she finished, "we've been trying to figure out how Ty's wife could have met my sister, and the only clue seems to be a meeting here. Bridget wrote that she attended it each week. Maybe Ty's wife came, too."

Ty shook his head. "It's not likely."

"It's all we have." Bri focused on the minister.

Tom tapped his finger against his chin. "I see. And when was this?"

"About a year ago. We're not sure of exact dates."

Once again the frustration rose. Bri watched Tyrel's face tighten up with nervousness. If only she'd kept better track of Bridget, paid more attention to her needs instead of spending all her time in the lab to get the details lined up for that dissertation. Maybe then she'd have known all the facts that Tyrel longed to hear.

A motion in the corner of her eye drew Briony's attention away from the handsome forester and back to the minister.

"Oh, that's too bad." Tom shook his head, his face sad. "There's no way, then. I'm sorry."

Bri frowned. "You don't remember her?"

"I'm afraid I don't. But then, I wouldn't. I'm new here, you see. Since last Christmas. I'm afraid I wouldn't have any information about your sister." He offered an apologetic smile to Ty. "Or your wife."

"It doesn't matter." Ty heaved himself to his feet, his face impassive.

But Briony could clearly read the message in the glance he telegraphed to her. *Why bother? There are no answers here.*

His hopelessness and despair ate at her confidence. This was a clue, she was certain of it. Years of conducting painstaking research and tracing every lead always yielded results. Why hadn't she stayed awake last night, pored over that book and found him some shred of hope?

Please, Lord. I need a little help. If he could just catch a glimpse of Your hand working, maybe he'd be able to trust just a little longer. Couldn't You just send me an idea?

Stalling for time, Bri shuffled to her feet, her mind working furiously. As she slowly pushed the stroller, her glance fell on the list tacked to a nearby bulletin board.

"Come on. Cristine will be awake soon." Ty stood in the doorway, shifting from one foot to the other. It was obvious he wanted out.

"The group." The glimmer in her brain grew. "Maybe someone in the group would remember her." She turned to the minister and begged with her eyes. "It might be worth a shot, don't you think?"

He nodded, contemplating the idea. "It might indeed. People come and go all the time, but someone may remember your sister." He chewed on his bottom lip. "I won't be able to ask them until next week, though."

"Next week?" Ty repeated.

Bri wanted this mystery solved as badly as anyone, so it came as no surprise when Ty blurted out his disappointment. But truth be told, she had far less at stake than him right now. Bridget had given her child to the

Demens by signing the adoption form and ensuring the paperwork was done correctly. But if she hadn't notified Cristine's biological father, Ty Demens's position could be threatened. Of course he was apprehensive!

She turned back to the minister. "We're very anxious to speak to anyone who might have known her."

"I understand." He patted her hand. "But the group only meets once a week. Some of them come from a distance and some have to make special work arrangements to be here."

"Maybe we could phone them, one by one." As soon as she said it, Bri knew it wouldn't work. Tom's words only confirmed her fears.

"I'm sorry. The membership is private. In fact, the group is closed to new members after the second week. Only those who keep up a regular attendance are allowed in, and we never divulge names. It would threaten the confidentiality, you see. No one would feel secure in sharing."

"Of course." Ty's arm curled under her elbow, his other hand gripping the stroller handle. "We never meant to suggest that you should break any confidence. Goodbye." He hurried his daughter down the hall, ending the discussion abruptly.

"I'll stop back in," Bri called over her shoulder as she followed Ty. "Thanks for your help."

They emerged into the afternoon sun, with Bri rushing to match Ty's long-legged pace. "Slow down," she puffed at last, too tired to keep it up. "Where is the fire?"

"Sorry." He slowed slightly after casting her one dark look. Then he stopped. He lifted his hands off the stroller. "I need to get back to work. I'd better go."

"Oh." She gulped, wondering at the anger she glimpsed in his eyes. "Is anything wrong?" she ventured, when he didn't immediately walk away.

"Yes!" Ty drew her off the walkway and onto the grass, pulling the stroller with him so that they were out of sight of curious onlookers. His face loomed mere inches from Bri's as he growled at her.

"I know I wasn't the best husband in the world. I failed at a lot of things. I probably didn't have the happily-ever-after kind of marriage you women always read about."

From the look on his face, Bri guessed his marriage was probably a long way from that.

"But there is no way I want to talk about it with a bunch of strangers on the off chance one of them knew Andrea or your sister and can explain what they *might have been* doing together."

Briony peered up at him. The flecks in his eyes stood out, showing his anger. But she saw something else there, too.

Embarrassment? What on earth did he have to be embarrassed about? Wasn't it Andrea, his wife, who had kept the details of the adoption from him?

Or was Tyrel Demens hiding something? Something that he hadn't shared with her. Something that made him afraid.

Bri reorganized the information she had in military precision, but the question would not disappear.

Was Ty worried about other people learning some secret?

Cristine stirred, then let out a whimper.

"She'll wake up soon. I'd better get back." Bri stepped forward, grasping the stroller handles firmly.

"I guess I'll see you when you've finished work," she murmured, keeping her eyes downcast.

"Yeah. I guess." Ty took one last look at his daughter, brushed the golden curls off her forehead. He leaned over to place a tender kiss across her eyelids, then sighed. "Bye." He headed down the street without a backward glance.

Briony walked back to the stone cottage slowly, her mind racing a hundred miles an hour.

"I believed him," she murmured, puzzling it out in her mind. "I accepted that everything he said was fact. But what if it wasn't? What if he's the one who's not telling the whole truth? What if he's hiding something?"

That didn't seem right. Ty seemed as upright and straight-shooting as anyone she'd ever met. And yet, it would explain his fear. It would explain why he seemed dogged by worry.

But what could possibly be so awful about his marriage that he didn't want anyone to know?

Bri rolled the stroller into the house, removed the smiling little girl and changed her diaper, before offering her a drink. Then she spread a blanket on the floor and sat next to little Cristine while she played with her toys.

"He loves this child," she said aloud. "Anyone can see that. He adores the ground she crawls on." She thought for a moment, remembering the sad look that washed over Ty's face whenever he spoke of Andrea.

"I believe he loved his wife, too. So what in the world would Ty Demens have to hide?"

The first day she'd met him, he'd been so certain that Andrea had told him the truth about Cristine. What if, by probing the relationship between Bridget and

Andrea, Bri had made him remember another time his wife had lied to him? Or was it simply that Ty didn't want to tarnish her memory by digging into a past that couldn't be altered?

Was she hurting him unnecessarily by being here, by uncovering secrets that might be better left alone?

Bri built a tower of blocks and watched as Cristine giggled her glee, knocking them over with a brush of her chubby hand.

What if Ty felt that something in his and Andrea's past could lead to questioning of the adoption, or of their ability to be parents?

Suddenly a dark thought clouded Briony's mind. *What if all her probing into the past cost him his daughter?*

She didn't know how it could happen, of course. Bridget had certainly taken steps to ensure that her baby stayed where she put her. But the fact remained that Bri didn't know the whole story.

"By poking at it all the time I'm hurting him," she whispered, the knowledge causing a pang in her heart. "And I don't want to hurt him. He's had too much pain already. He and Cristine deserve to be happy together."

It didn't really matter what had happened. Briony knew Bridget, knew the kind of awful things she'd done when they were kids. And yet, she'd loved her sister in spite of it all.

"Perhaps Ty can't bear for his love for Andrea to be put to that test. Perhaps he wants to keep the image he has of her intact, unblemished."

Who was Briony Green to question his wishes?

For the next three hours Bri tossed the problem around in her mind as she played with Cristine, read her a story and took her for another short walk. Ty arrived home just as Bri had almost finished feeding the little girl her dinner.

"Hi." She studied his face anew. It was an honest face. That devoted look when he studied his daughter wasn't fake.

Bri made up her mind. Whatever was wrong, she wouldn't add to his pain. Her investigations would have to wait, or at least bypass him.

"Is anything wrong?" Ty placed his knapsack on a chair and hunkered down to tickle Cristine, whispering sweet nothings as he nuzzled against her neck. The little girl giggled and wiggled with sheer pleasure. He looked up from his play and caught Bri staring.

"Briony? Has something happened?"

When she didn't speak, he picked Cristine up out of her chair, holding her tightly in his protective embrace as his eyes scoured Bri's face.

"What is it?"

"It's nothing. I just wanted to let you know that I'm not going to be sticking my nose into your past anymore." Bri smiled to reassure him. "We scientists sometimes get caught up in digging for the truth. I can see that asking so many questions, puzzling over the past, hurts you," she said honestly.

"I see." He stared at her, his dark gaze roiling with confusion. "Why did you decide this?"

"When I look at Cristine, see how sweetly she smiles, how her eyes light up whenever you're around, I realize that the past and my sister's reason for being here, for choosing you—none of that matters." She brushed her hand over Cristine's bare foot, then her eyes rose to meet Ty's.

"This is what matters. The present and the future

for this sweet little soul. Anyone with eyes can see that she'll be perfectly happy with you, Ty. Nothing else compares to that.''

Ty studied Bri for a long time.

Eventually he set Cristine in her chair, straightened her bib and waited for Bri to resume feeding. Once the baby had begun slurping up bits of peach with pudgy fingers, Tyrel pulled off his tie, unbuttoned the neck of his shirt and raked one hand through his hair so that it stood straight up.

''That's where you're wrong, Miss Green. Dead wrong.''

His glacial voice sent her head jerking upward in surprise. Her eyes met his, searching for an answer.

''I don't understand,'' she whispered, aghast at the agony that pulled his handsome features taut.

''Cristine's past may well affect her future in a way that none of us can control, unless we prepare for it.'' He raised a hand when she would have spoken. ''I know you're concerned for me and that's very noble of you, but believe me, I can take it.'' His mouth creased in a wry grin. ''I figured out this afternoon that I can handle anything that we may discover, so long as it means my daughter's future is with me.''

Briony hated to say it, knew how much it would hurt him. But she had to ask, had to know. ''And if it isn't?'' she whispered.

He stood ramrod straight, his shoulders thrust back, his chin jutted out. It was his combat stance.

How wonderful to be loved like that, Briony marveled. How incredible to know that you had someone on your side who would stand behind you no matter what.

Ty's words snapped out in harsh resolve. ''Cristine's future is with me. There's no discussion about that. But I need to be prepared. I need every bit of information there is out there, good or bad. Can you understand?'' His eyes beseeched her.

"I have to do everything in my power to ensure no one will take her away. So if you have to dig into the past, dig. As long as it helps me keep Cristine, I don't care about anything else. Her welfare is primary.''

She stared at him, awed by the fierceness in his voice. At the corner of his eye, a bit of moisture glimmered in the light. Bri swallowed, hard.

"And if I find something unpleasant?'' she said at last.

"You keep digging,'' he told her. "Whatever my wife did, she had a good reason. I'd like to know what that reason was.'' A bleakness washed over his face, then disappeared.

His fingers closed around Bri's arm, forcing her to look at him.

"Do you hear me, Briony? Talk to people, ask questions, find out all you can. And if I ever again tell you to stop, ignore me. I need to know the truth. Cristine deserves it.''

"The truth often hurts,'' she reminded him.

"I've been hurt before.'' His voice crackled with ice. "I'll live. As long as you don't lie to me, I'll be fine.''

"I'll never lie to you,'' Bri promised solemnly.

But as she walked home half an hour later, she wondered how dearly that promise would cost him.

And her.

Chapter Four

A few days later, Briony took advantage of the baby's naptime to do some household organizing and review the information she had thus far.

It wasn't much.

Bridget's diary was slow reading. So many of the entries revealed a longing for God's love. Often Briony had to put it away, lest her emotion blind her to the information she was seeking. She had gained only one clue so far. Bridget cared deeply about the opinion of a man named Kent.

"I need to find him," she told herself, setting the last of the spices on the shelf.

That's when she realized she'd just emptied and then refilled Ty's cupboards using the precise alphabetical method she'd used in her own apartment. "At least he'll find everything quicker." She hoped.

She was thankful that the phone rang, so she didn't have to rationalize it all out.

"Hello?"

"How is my granddaughter?"

"Mrs. Demens!" Bri smiled into the phone. "I should be asking how you are."

"Bored silly," the older woman complained. "All I do is sit around and crochet. My daughter won't let me do a thing except watch the flowers grow. I wish I were there with you and Cristine."

"We do, too." Sometimes Bri desperately wished someone was here to confide in, to reassure her that her mistakes wouldn't permanently harm Cristine.

"Are you finding it too difficult?"

The soft-voiced concern soothed Bri's battered heart. Maybe she wasn't so alone.

"I usually end up putting her outfits on backward," Briony admitted. "When Ty comes home, he always changes them around with this strange glower, as if he's fed up with my stupidity." She gulped, then decided to say what was in her heart.

"It's not that I'm not trying, Mrs. Demens. But reason tells me the buttons and snaps should be in the front to make it easier to change her. I listened and tried to do as he did. The one time I put them in the back, I was wrong then, too. It's so confusing and totally illogical."

"Oh, dear." It sounded as though Monica Demens was laughing.

"The only time I get it right is when she wears a dress."

"Is Cristine happy?"

"She seems all right. She giggles and laughs most of the time she's awake." A warmth flooded Bri's heart. "She's got a funny little smile that she uses when she makes this particular shriek. I think she's teasing me."

"If you were doing something wrong, she wouldn't

be smiling," Mrs. Demens pointed out. "Stop worrying so much. I'm sure Ty thinks you're doing a marvelous job. He seemed quite pleased when I spoke to him last night."

"Did he?" Bri could hardly imagine it. "Well, I'm trying, even though I feel like a fish out of water."

"You'll do fine, dear. And remember, I'm praying for you."

"Thank you. I can use that."

"Have you, er, found out any more about your sister?"

Bri swallowed. She'd felt Ty's irritation with the subject on several occasions and had learned to keep her own counsel.

"Not much. I've been trying to dig into her diary, but the company who hired me also asked me to do a little preliminary reading on some studies they've already conducted, so my evenings have been pretty full."

"I can imagine. Don't overdo, Briony. Whatever the truth of the past, Cristine is healthy and happy and has a family that truly loves her. I don't think anything can change that."

Bri nodded. "I know. I just want everything cleared up before I have to leave. I want to make sure nothing can change Bridget's plans or take Cristine from Ty. Then I'll be satisfied."

After a few more minutes of chatter, Mrs. Demens said, "I'd love to drive out for a chat, Briony, but my daughter lives on the far side of Calgary and she works such full days. Asking her to drive an hour-and-a-half into Banff for a little visit then turn around to go home seems so demanding, especially after all she's already done for me."

"But you're supposed to keep your leg up! You can't do that in a car." Bri hurried to reassure her. "We're fine. Truly."

"I'm glad." A faint sigh. "Things seem so rushed here. I guess I'd gotten used to the serenity of the park. Giselle and her husband are always on the run to soccer and baseball games."

"That must be lonely for you."

"Actually, I rather enjoy the calm after the storm." Mrs. Demens laughed. "You'd have to know Giselle to understand, Briony. She's like a whirlwind that just can't sit still. I shouldn't complain so much."

"Sometimes we just have to share, don't we?" Bri wished she had someone she could share with. She'd never been really good with people. Perhaps that's what made it so easy to fall back into her books and studies.

"If you're looking for a friend, you can't do worse than Ty's church. Such a lot of dedicated young souls. They're really friendly."

"I'll try it on Sunday, if Ty doesn't need me," Bri said. "I'm not ready to take a child to church just yet— Oops, there's Cristine. I'd better go. She doesn't like to be kept waiting."

"How well I remember!" Mrs. Demens laughed. "I'll be praying." Then she said goodbye.

Bri hung up and climbed the stairs to the little girl's room. "Thanks," she whispered. "I can use all the help I can get."

Once Cristine was changed, she was raring to go. Unfortunately an earlier light mist had now turned into a steady drizzle that diminished the options for playtime.

Bri checked over her baby-care schedule and knew

there was no way around it. Cristine needed this free time to work off her energy. If Cristine didn't get enough exercise, the little girl turned into an imp.

Briony surveyed the living room, crowded with furniture, playpen, baby swing and a host of plush toys that spilled all over everything. The chaotic mess irritated her more now than ever before.

Time for a change.

"Cristine, my love, you just sit in here for a minute while Auntie Bri makes you a play space."

She popped the little girl in the playpen, rolled up the sleeves of her crisp white blouse and began shifting things around until the furniture was arranged around the periphery of the room and Cristine's play blanket and toys sat in the center.

"Now you've got lots of room to toddle, if you want." Bri hugged the powdery-soft body close until Cristine wriggled to get down. "And no tables to bump this nose."

Cristine immediately tested the theory by rushing across the carpet as fast as her chubby little legs would carry her. She smacked into the cushions of the sofa, sat down with a thump and grinned.

"You like that, huh?" Bri moved the swing out of the way, behind the love seat. Then she tossed the extra toys into the playpen, while Cristine fiddled with the toy lawn mower that purred when she thrust it across the floor, gobbling up anything in its path.

"You and I think alike, my dear."

Bri stood, watching the little girl babble as she played with her toys. If Ty wanted to entertain, all he had to do was remove the playpen full of toys, and the room would look like a normal living room again.

"Except for those awful towels." She leaned down

to tuck yet another edge under the cushion. "I suppose they're to protect this thing from your drooling," she mumbled, tickling Cristine. "But they're always coming off."

Cristine apparently agreed, for she began to tug on one corner. When it finally pulled free, she pulled the towel over her head and giggled.

"Peek-a-boo." Bri knew this game. She dragged the towel off and grinned. "There you are."

Off came the next towel, and the next, until the furniture sat completely uncovered.

"We'll leave it that way for a while, sweetie, but I've got to put them back before your dad comes home."

"No." Cristine mowed the towels, sturdy little legs propelling her across the room.

"I wish you'd learn another word," Bri told her, crouching down to pick up the towels.

"No." Cristine tugged one free and mowed it again. "No."

"How about 'yes,' Cristine? Yes, yes, yes."

"No." She pulled on the drooping edge. "No."

"You win." Bri let the entire bundle drop. "If your dad gets angry with me again, I'm going to tell him Cristine made me do it."

"No."

Bri shook her head and collapsed on the floor, her back against the sofa. It was going to be one of "those" afternoons.

By five-thirty Briony was ready to dial 911.

"Cristine, this is good. Mmm. Potatoes are nice. Here, see?" She pretended to eat some off the tiny baby spoon. "Mmm." She held the spoon to Cristine's lips.

Cristine opened her mouth for just one reason. "No." Her eyes darkened, her chin jerked up and her tiny feet pummeled the footrest on the high chair. "No!" she bellowed shoving the spoon directly into Briony's shirt.

"Cristine—"

The little girl shape-shifted right before her eyes. Gone was the sulky look, the angry tilt to sweet pink lips. Bri gaped, stunned by the sudden change in the child. Cristine dropped her hands, her face lost its furious red tinge and a huge smile transformed her face.

"Mmm." Cristine held up her arms. "Up."

"Hey, sweetie." Ty swung through the door, his face lighting up at the sight of the child. He bent down to brush a kiss over her potato-laden hair. "You look pretty grubby, kiddo." His scrutiny moved to Bri.

Bri looked grubby, too. She knew he itched to say it.

Her braids had come loose and bits of hair now drooped and clung to her face and neck in the messiest way. Most of Cristine's lunch and almost all of her dinner clung to Bri's body in various spots, including her shoes.

"Don't hold back on my account," she muttered.

"You look worse than she does," Ty told her bluntly as he picked a pea out of her hair. "What're we having, a food fight?"

Bri kept her smile with great difficulty. "She's not happy about staying inside today." Which was the understatement of the year! The most rigorous day of research had never left Bri as drained as she felt right now.

"So why didn't you take her outside?" He stood frowning as she scooped potato off herself.

"It's been raining."

"She won't melt. It's far better for her to get some fresh air than to be cooped up inside all day. Next time put her coat on and take her out."

It hurt to be criticized when none of it was her fault. Bri knew she wasn't good at baby-sitting. She often felt uncertain and useless. Cristine seemed to understand that, for she chose just those moments to act up.

"I'll clean her up and go," she murmured, blinking away the rush of tears that blurred her vision. She took a washcloth and held it beneath the tap. "I think she's eaten all she wants for the moment."

"Good thing, too. Another ten minutes and we'd have total destruction." He tweaked the little girl's ear, then hurried away to change out of his uniform.

Cristine was not thrilled with being left in her chair, and she fought Bri's efforts to remove the food as hard as Bri fought to keep her emotions in check.

What was wrong with her? Bri had never been emotional; she hated that kind of display. She liked to assess the situation completely and then act accordingly. But this situation continually tested her theories and her logic. Neither seemed to work with the miniature bundle of energy in front of her.

"Come on, Cristine. We've got to get this mess cleaned up if you're going to see Daddy. Hold out your hand." Bri forcibly unfolded the little fingers and wiped away the mush inside. "Good girl," she muttered. "Now the other one."

"No!" Cristine grabbed a few loose strands of Bri's hair and yanked for all she was worth.

It was the last straw in a long and trying day. Bri backed away, her hand to her aching head, fighting to keep the tears from coursing down her cheeks.

"What happened to the living room?" Ty Demens sauntered into the kitchen, clean, pressed and frowning. "Why is the furniture rearranged?"

"Cristine needs more room to move around." Bri turned her back on him, huddling over the sink as the tears welled in her eyes. Her scalp stung like crazy, and now she had a headache, too. She gulped, made her voice firm. "If she runs, she bumps into the table. I tried to give her room to move."

"It's kind of awkward coming down the stairs," he told her with a growl. "I banged my shin on the swing."

"Sorry." It was the best apology she could scrape together.

Bri concentrated on washing the pans that wouldn't fit in the already full dishwasher. Most of them came from Ty's dinner creation of the night before, and she'd had to soak them all day to get the spaghetti sauce and burned meat loose.

Finally she had the entire mess scrubbed and draining on the board. She wiped down the counter with a sigh.

"Hey, Cris. You're all mucky. I think you need a bath." Ty's voice brimmed with love as he spoke to the now cooing child. "Briony, are you almost finished with the sink?"

"Yes, almost." Bri surreptitiously dried her eyes with the dish towel, scoured the last pot halfheartedly and then began stowing everything in the neat precise style she'd arranged earlier.

"Hey, what's this? I can't find her shampoo." Ty began hauling things out of the cupboard with no regard for their arrangement.

"Stop it!" Bri could no more have stifled that response than she could have made her hands move from her fierce clasp around his arm. "I spent half the morning organizing that. Kindly don't undo my work!"

He blinked. "But nothing's where it's supposed to be."

"It's all in order. Cristine's things are here, in this cupboard near the sink so you can reach them easily while bathing her. Her bathtub is under the sink, where it's out of the way."

"What was wrong with the way it was?" He jammed his hands on his hips belligerently.

"It wasn't that it was wrong, exactly. It's just more efficient this way."

"Huh?"

Bri felt a slow burn creep up her neck. "It is more efficient to do it this way. If everything has a place and is kept in it, things can be done in half the time. I spent forty minutes searching for the dish detergent this morning. It didn't occur to me you kept it in the bathroom."

He grinned. "I don't. I was using it to clean my binocular lenses."

"And Cristine's diapers? I found the new box in the broom closet."

"I always keep them there."

"Why? Wouldn't it make more sense to keep them in her room?"

He shrugged, his eyes wide with confusion. "I guess. I just go get them when I need them."

"When I needed them, I didn't have time to go hunting." She decided not to tell him that she'd used one of his T-shirts as a stop-gap measure.

"You're making this into a big deal." He yanked out the tub and flopped it on the counter, adding water as he continued. "It's not as if I'm totally disorganized. I've been doing this for fifteen months and I think I've managed pretty well."

Now who was criticizing? Bri took a deep breath, handed Cristine a biscuit and then scrubbed down her high chair.

"I'm sure you've done a wonderful job, Ty. It's just that this is all new to me." She straightened the cupboard he'd messed, then stood. "I'm used to working in a lab. If you want a swab, you go to the place where swabs are kept. Then you get back to what you were doing."

"This isn't a lab, it's a home," he countered, opening and closing drawers until he found the one where she'd laid the baby's bath towels.

"That doesn't mean we can't utilize a system of order." She lifted the baby out of the high chair and stripped her clothes off before setting her in the bath. "You see, I can hold her with this hand and reach everything I need without losing my grip."

To demonstrate, Bri handed Cristine the rubber duck from the window ledge, squirted out a tiny bit of shampoo from the bottle she'd set on a nearby shelf, and then washed it off, all without letting go of the slippery little girl.

"It's safer," she murmured stepping back when his hands closed around the child's soft skin. She watched him for a few moments.

"I was trying to do the same thing in the living room," she murmured. "I wasn't trying to disrupt your system or imply you weren't doing your best."

When Ty didn't say anything, she gathered up her briefcase, shoved in the information she'd organized about her sister and stepped toward the door.

"I've got to get going. I promised someone I'd meet them and I'll be late if I don't hurry." Avoiding Ty, Bri managed to brush a kiss across the baby's cheek. "Bye, sweetie. See you Monday." Then she hurried out the door, closing it firmly behind her.

As she stepped outside, Bri thought she heard him call her name. But she didn't stop. Instead, she hurried toward her favorite spot by the river. Thankfully the little wooden bench was empty, though tourists strolled past constantly.

She collapsed onto the bench and stared out over the rippling water, absorbing the peace and serenity with every pore. Now and then a trout jumped up to catch a fly. The rain had long since stopped, leaving the trees, wildflowers and grassy bank glistening, as if God had just finished dusting.

Ty made her feel as if she were a child again—a misfit, an oddball. Now, as she sat watching, Bri felt awkward and out of step with the rest of the world. All around her couples held hands, whispering, laughing, sharing the beauty together.

As usual, she sat on the outside looking in.

"You gave Bridget peace and solace here," she whispered to the pink-kissed sky. "Can't you do the same for me? I like structure and orderliness. I was just trying to help. Why is that always wrong?"

Cars rumbled past on the stone bridge to her left. In the mist of evening shadows it looked like the troll bridge from Cristine's book of fairy tales. Across the river, a mother elk with her baby munched on the long grass, tail swishing in perfect four-four time. Every so often the mother lifted her head and stared at Bri. Then she went back to chewing.

"Hi. I'm sorry I'm late. I'm Sandi Harker."

Bri glanced up, surprised.

"From the hotel? We talked on the phone yesterday."

"Yes, of course. I'm so glad you could meet me so quickly, especially since I only found your name in my sister's diary last night," Bri apologized. "I guess I just got lost in thought."

"Good place to do it." Sandi flipped her black shorn head back with a grin. "Bridget used to come here quite a lot."

"She did?" The knowledge cheered Bri somehow, made her feel not quite so alone. "Did you know my sister well?"

Sandi shrugged. "Not that well. We roomed together for a while, then Kent helped her get her own place."

Bri sat up straight. "You knew Kent?"

"I knew who he was. Lots of people did." Sandi snapped her gum, her eyes busy assessing the outlandish costume of an Alpine yodeler. "Look at them. Anything for the tourists' dollars. Pathetic!"

Briony couldn't have cared less about the man, but she couldn't let the criticism go.

"He's not out for a dollar. He's here from Austria. There's a yodeling contest in Lake Louise, I think he said." She grinned at Sandi's stare. "We're staying at the same bed-and-breakfast."

"Oh. Anyway, like I said, lots of people knew Kent. Not many liked him."

"Why not?" At last she was finding out something about the man Bridget had cared for.

"He was a creep."

"A creep? What do you mean?" Dread niggled at her. She'd been so afraid of this, so worried that Cristine's father would be the kind one didn't want to tell one's child about.

"He was, like, preaching all the time. You know." Sandi snapped her gum while she sought the appropriate words. "You gotta be saved because Jesus loves you, an' all that stuff. He just kept harping on it."

"Oh." What relief! Bri couldn't stop the grin of joy. "I was afraid Bridget had hooked up with someone into drugs or something."

Sandi frowned. "Maybe she did. I wouldn't know about that."

"Do you know where I could find this Kent? What his last name is?" Hope kept Bri from breathing.

"Sure." Sandi nodded. "Kent Young. Usually teaches up at Sunshine in the winter. He's on the ski patrol there, too."

"And in the summer? Now? What does he do in the off season?" Anticipation shivered over the nerves in her fingers as she clutched her briefcase close. "Do you know, Sandi?"

Sandi frowned. "I think he went to Africa or somewhere on some mission trip. Building churches, maybe?"

Briony closed her eyes as hope drained away. She was normally a patient person, willing to wait whatever time it took to get results. But Cristine's parentage was in question. For Ty's sake, she'd wanted it all cleared up.

"You wouldn't know how I could reach him?" she asked hopefully, then sighed at Sandi's negative response. "I didn't think so."

"Why do you want to talk to Kent so bad? Is something wrong?" Sandi snapped nonchalantly, her eyes curious.

"Not wrong, really. But as the father of Bridget's baby, he should have signed off on the adoption." Bri tented her fingers together, then let them fall into her lap.

"Kent? The baby's father?" Sandi burst into loud laughter. "No way! He preached all the time about how sex before marriage was a problem the world didn't need. That kind of stuff was his favorite sermon." She snapped again, her black head twisting from side to side.

"No way!" she repeated, then she winked. "Besides, Bridget was pregnant before she met him."

"She was?" Bri didn't know what to think. This was more information than she'd dared hope to gain. She didn't like asking these questions of a virtual stranger, of course, but she had to know. She'd have to go back over the few pages she'd read, try to find some other answer. "She wrote so much about Kent that I figured..."

"You figured wrong. I don't know who the father was, but last time I saw her, I got the impression she was done with the guy. She was pretty upset."

Sandi had to go. Bri thanked her, offered to buy her lunch another time, and watched the girl walk away, jaws snapping in time to her feet.

With a tired sigh, Bri lugged the briefcase off the bench and started toward the bed-and-breakfast.

"Back to square one," she muttered to herself. "Thank goodness tomorrow's Saturday. I can get a chance to really dig in to the diary. There's got to be a clue somewhere. There's just got to be, God. Ty needs to know for certain that his rights won't be challenged."

But that wasn't the only reason Bri wanted to know more.

I've got to get out of his house, she thought several hours later, as she sat on the window seat and watched the mountain sky fill with stars. *I'm getting too involved. I'm getting too close to Cristine. I have to remember that she's not mine. She won't ever be mine.*

The moon flickered out from behind a silvery-gray cloud, daring her to tell the truth.

"But she could have been," she whispered to the darkness. "I would have cared for your daughter, Bridget. If only you had let me know."

The hurt blossomed inside.

"I'm trying to be satisfied, Lord," she whispered as the tears she'd kept bottled up for so long finally rolled down her cheeks. "Please help me to be content with whatever You give."

This time the peace was a long time coming.

Chapter Five

"Your father is a jerk, Cristine Demens. A first-class, award-winning jerk."

Cristine grinned her agreement, her pudgy hands battering Ty's chest as if to punish him. She shrilled her delight as the Saturday morning cartoons flickered across the television.

"So what's the next step, kiddo? Got any ideas?"

It wasn't that Ty didn't know the answer. His mother had spent the past fourteen months complaining about his habit of pushing too hard, riding roughshod over others to get his own will done. She hadn't minced any words, either.

"'Do something or get out of the way' is not a philosophy that will win you friends, my boy," she'd told him only last week when he'd complained about someone at work. "It's about time you learn that there are some people in this world who simply refuse to be pushed into doing things your way, no matter how right you think you are."

From the glare she directed his way, Ty got the impression she was one of those people.

Judging by the precise organization of his house, Briony Green was another. Look at the way she'd arranged the spice rack.

"Alphabetical spices?" He rolled his eyes at Cristine. "Who arranges their spices alphabetically?"

"Bee." Cristine blinked her big blue eyes, staring at him like a wise owl. "Bee." She wiggled to get down off his chest. "Bee," she yelled again, tottering over to her stroller.

Ty let her go, his mind busy reviewing the previous evening.

As he watched, his daughter knocked his coffee cup over, drenching the sofa—which no longer bore the protective towel coverings.

Ty sighed and mopped up the mess with a perfectly folded rag from the neatly arranged linen closet. Was the woman going to chart and graph his entire life?

Not that it should have mattered what the provocation was. Ty knew he'd hurt her feelings, had complained when he should have been on his hands and knees thanking her. He closed his eyes and winced at the memory.

He'd have to apologize to Briony, and sooner would be better than later. Maybe something would come to him out by the lake. Ty got up to finish what he'd started, thrusting Briony Green and her penchant for order out of his mind.

"Bee."

"What's that, kitten?" Ty placed the last of the lunch he'd prepared inside the picnic basket, quickly slid in a bottle of juice for Cristine and two others for himself. "There, that should hold us."

"Bee." Cristine wasn't giving up easily. Whatever this new word meant, she wanted it. Now.

"Ready to go fishing, sweetie? A nice fat pickerel would be good for dinner, wouldn't it?" Where had he tossed her jacket last night after stomping up and down the streets trying to get her to sleep? "Here we are." He tugged it from behind the high chair, conscience pricking him.

Briony was right. Organization beat bedlam any day. He was organized at work. Why was it so hard at home? One look at the kitchen she'd left pristine last night and he understood. He was a slob because his mother had let him get away with it.

"I'll start making the change tonight. Okay, sweet pea?" He swung the little girl up high in his arms, catching her when she let out a peal of giggles. "That's better. Come on, baby girl. Let's go fishing."

"Bee."

"Well, you might see some bees." He hoped that would satisfy her. It didn't. Ty spent far longer than he should have loading fishing gear, a picnic basket and one small child into his Jeep. He was tired by the time they pulled out of the yard. No wonder Bri had rushed away last night!

Ty turned right twice and was heading down Banff's main street when Cristine resumed her complaints from the back seat.

"Bee," she yelled, fists pounding on her car seat. "Bee!" It was a demand he couldn't ignore.

Ty turned his head to say something, and caught a glimpse of Briony as she strolled down the sidewalk. For the first time since the day she'd shown up at his door, she had let her hair down. Now it flowed in a river of gold to well below her shoulders.

"Bee! Bee!"

Briony. *Bee.* Ty pulled over to the curb and turned to grin at the red-faced child behind him.

"Bee," she yelled again and pointed. "Bee."

"I've got it, honey. Stop screaming." He leaned over the passenger seat and called through the open window. "Good morning, Briony."

She stopped immediately, but waited a few minutes before she turned and acknowledged him. Her eyes were cool glacial blue, maybe even frostbitten.

"Bee. Bee." Cristine was jerking back and forth in her seat, trying to get out.

When a host of Japanese tourists turned to frown at his screeching daughter, Briony took pity on him, crossed the sidewalk and leaned in the window.

"Good morning. Hello, Cristine." She reached over to squeeze the little hand. "How are you today?"

"Bee."

Briony glanced at him, one eyebrow arched.

"I think it's her name for you. She's been yelling it for almost ten minutes." Ty shifted behind the wheel, wondering how he was going to sneak in an apology without admitting his off-the-cuff method didn't work.

"Really?" Bri's face lit up, the ice melted and her eyes glowed a brilliant blue. "A new word? And she used it to call me?"

"I think so."

Briony pulled the back door open and slid across the seat to hug the little girl. "Sweetie, that's wonderful. A new word!"

Ty noticed the way Briony winced, then carefully edged away from the curious hands that grabbed for her hair. Like a movie, his mind reversed tape to last

night and the long blond hairs his daughter had
clutched while he bathed her.

Cristine had pulled her hair, hard enough to loosen
a baby fist full of the glossy gold. It must have hurt
incredibly. He could have kicked himself for his ig-
norance.

Bri had spent a long, hard, *thankless* day with his
very demanding daughter, and he'd added to her stress
by complaining about a couple of pieces of furniture
and some cupboards. What a jerk!

For the first time Ty began to visualize what acting
as caregiver had done to Briony's world. Everything
about her was fastidiously correct, in place, catego-
rized and classified. But nothing was meticulous, organized or reasonable when it came to a child. He'd
had fifteen months to figure that out, but he'd expected
Briony to know it from the start. Why? Because she
was a woman?

Ty closed his eyes and swallowed. Had he become
what his sister always claimed—a bossy boor?

Just yesterday he'd seen copies of three bestselling
baby books tumbling out of the briefcase Bri always
brought along. She had probably read them all, even
believed it when they listed the frequency with which
Cristine would need to be fed, changed, played with.
Unfortunately, Cristine had never read the books!

Ty could have groaned at his pigheaded stubborn-
ness, but that wouldn't have done any good.

What he did do was apologize.

"I'm really sorry about my bad attitude last night,
Briony. Please feel free to make whatever changes you
think will be best for Cristine. You're doing a wonderful thing for us, and I have no right to question or

complain about any of it. I'm just so thankful you're there for her.''

"It's your house. I should have checked first." Her voice oozed studious politeness. She refused to look at him, busy with Cristine and a game of pat-a-cake.

Ty reached over the seat and put his hand on hers, stilling the game. She had to look at him then.

"No, Briony, you shouldn't have to check at all. And I don't want you to feel you do. You're in charge. Feel free to change whatever you like. Okay?" He sat, waiting, hoping.

Long pause. "All right. Thank you."

"And you'll forgive me for being so cranky?"

She smiled grimly. "Everyone gets tired."

"That wasn't tiredness. That was sheer bad manners. Cristine reminded me of it this morning." He had her attention now.

"Cristine did?"

He could see her trying to reason it out, sift out the facts and line them all up in neat, precise rows. Apparently they didn't compute. She frowned.

"How could Cristine do that?"

Ty wanted to laugh. She was so methodical, so predictable. He suddenly itched to show her that there was a whole world of things she was missing out on by being so analytical.

"Cristine thumped me on the chest this morning. And she wasn't playing around. You know how outspoken my daughter can be."

"Trust me, I do know that." She grinned at him.

Ty couldn't breath, he couldn't swallow. He could only stare. Why, she was gorgeous! When Briony Green forgot to be so reserved and polite, her true radiance shone through.

"I know this is your day off, and feel free if you want to say no, but I was wondering if you'd like to come along with us. We're going fishing." Now what had made him invite her on his favorite, most longed-for escape?

"I don't think so. I don't know how to fish." She beat a quick retreat into her shell again, blond head shaking a definite no.

"Don't know how to fish, huh?" He copped an amazed stare. "You visit Banff and don't fish? I don't think so."

She frowned at him.

"I'll help you. It's simple. You throw in the hook, they bite—bingo! You fish." Suddenly he wanted to show her that he wasn't the sourpuss he'd acted all week.

"I somehow don't think I'd be very good at it. I could watch Cristine for you, though." She straightened Cristine's sunhat and retied one shoe.

"Nope." He wasn't going to let her get away with it. "Cristine doesn't need a sitter today. She just needs to see her auntie Bee."

"Bee," Cristine yelled in support.

Briony burst out in startled laughter. "All right," she agreed at last, holding up her hands in mock surrender, "I'd love to go with you. Fishing it is."

He insisted she climb into the front seat, and before Cristine's angry bellows could change her mind, he steered out of the town and onto the overpass.

"I suppose you have a secret fishing place," she murmured, reaching back to bind her hair into a wide barrette. The golden strands burst out and down her back like a geyser.

"Briony, I'm very sorry Cristine pulled your hair,"

he murmured, forcing his eyes back to the road. "It must have stung."

"How did you know?" Briony averted her gaze.

"She was clutching a fist of that gold of yours when I bathed her. I'm afraid it only clicked when I saw you with your hair loose." He swallowed, unable to tear his eyes from her. "It's very beautiful hair."

Her head jerked around, her eyes huge as she peered at him. "My hair is beautiful?" she squeaked.

Ty frowned. What was this about? Briony seemed totally unaware of the striking picture she made sitting in his truck in her navy chinos and matching navy shirt. She was all cool efficiency, brimming with capability.

Compared to her, he was all thumbs. As she lifted one perfectly pressed sleeve to remove a bit of something from Cristine's jacket, Ty remembered the state of his kitchen and winced. Better not to think about it right now.

"Your hair is lovely," he repeated. "Don't you like it?"

"I—I never really thought about it." Her cheeks sported matching flags of hot pink. "Braiding it keeps it out of the way, but sometimes my scalp gets sore and I have to wear it down."

"It's very nice down. And up." He barely caught the flash of pleasure in her eyes before she ducked her head.

"Th-thank you."

"You're welcome." He turned off the highway and onto a gravel road. "How long did it take you to get your doctorate?"

"A year longer than it should have." With that one sentence her face closed up, all pleasure drained away.

Now what had he done?

"I'm sorry. I didn't mean to pry."

She said nothing.

Ty sighed. He'd been a fool to ask her to come. It was going to be a long day.

"This project you're going to be working on—" He tried again. Surely she wasn't touchy about work. "What's behind it?"

"With the number of tourists and vehicles traveling in the parks these days, diseases are spread far quicker than they would have if left to themselves."

Ah, now she was in her comfort zone. Ty drove, listening as she explained how she hoped to genetically alter some of the species currently being damaged.

Then the talk turned technical, and he got lost. Fortunately, Cristine didn't like being ignored.

"Bee."

Ty couldn't help but stare as Bri emerged from her technical world. It was like watching Sleeping Beauty wake up. Briony blinked, her eyes opened wide and she glanced around the Jeep as if she'd never seen it before. The baby yelled again, bringing her world back into focus. A funny smile tugged at her lips. She turned, checked Cristine.

"I'm sorry. I was babbling. I tend to forget that not everyone is as enthused as I am on this subject." Her face glowed bright red as she stared out the window. Her hands knotted in her lap. "Sorry to bore you."

Bore him? It was obvious to Ty that Briony carried scars from her past. She'd mentioned before that her sister was different. It wasn't that difficult to imagine some remembered hurt from their past echoing through her mind.

"I guess it would be boring to someone who didn't

make their living from the trees and the forest," he assured her quietly. "But I wasn't bored. Sometime I'd like to see your facility."

"Really?"

There it was again, that soft inner light that infused her skin with a breathtaking luminosity.

"Perhaps after I've been there for a while, you and Cristine could come for a visit."

Ty laughed. "Somehow I can't quite see Cristine placidly looking around a lab. Can you?"

Her lips curved in a tender smile, which she bestowed on the babbling little girl. "Well, maybe not."

"Definitely not." He braked the vehicle and waved a hand at the vista before them. "This is Cristine's kind of lab."

"It's gorgeous."

Ty was certain Briony wasn't even aware she'd left the truck. She stepped into the meadow, face thrust into the sunshine as she surveyed the blue-green water and surrounding grassy meadow.

"It's a perfect playground," he heard her whisper. "She chooses well."

"Bee!" Cristine's urgent summons forced Ty to abandon his study of the small blond professor.

"Come on, darling. It's playtime."

Cristine bounced and jiggled in the car seat, smiling like a cat offered cream when she spied the water. "Up, up!"

"I'm trying, honey. Just settle down."

At last he had her free. Ty couldn't help his grin of pure pride at the way his daughter charged ahead, intent on catching up to Briony.

It took a few minutes to unload the truck, spread out an old quilt and organize his fishing stuff. He'd play with Cristine first, he decided. Then, when she was tuckered out, he'd cast a line and contemplate.

Cristine wasn't waiting. She'd already tugged off her shoes and now thrust one fat toe into the lake, screaming with delight at the chill. Ty poised on his toes, ready to charge forward, until he saw Bri crouch down beside the little girl. She'd also removed her shoes, he realized, surprised by the move. Her pants were rolled up past her knees, and she, too, dabbled in the water.

He walked over slowly, enjoying the picture of the two of them, so fair against the vivid water. They could have passed for mother and daughter.

As fast as it came, Ty thrust the thought away, anger burning in a tight hot spot deep inside. His daughter didn't have a mother. God had taken her away in some kind of cruel divine joke. Fine, he'd deal with that. But no one, including an aunt who made him feel things he shouldn't, or some biological father who'd never even met her, was going to part him from his little girl.

He'd play the hand he was given. Alone.

"Going swimming?" Two shining heads twisted to grin at him. "It's still pretty cold." He held out Cristine's pail and shovel. "How about if we build something?"

"A sand castle?" Briony cast a dubious glance at the coarse beach. "I don't think it will work."

"She hasn't any faith in us, sweet pea." Ty picked up Cristine and whirled her around. "She doesn't know that we can build something out of anything. Shall we demonstrate?"

Cristine babbled her response and squirmed to get down. Ty let her go, pail in hand, to gather whatever treasures she deemed appropriate. She didn't wander far, but he kept his eyes glued to her, anyway.

"You're very good with her." Briony smiled as Cristine dumped her pile of stones at Ty's feet. "I'm glad Bridget chose you as her family."

"No more doubts about her safety?"

Bri smiled, her face soft, reminiscent.

"Actually, I didn't have any doubts after the first hour," she said. "I just pretended I did because I wanted to get to know her. She's so precious."

"You'll be a good mother to your own kids one day," he murmured, piling stone upon stone with Cristine's help. "You're patient, calm, loving—all the things a child needs."

The silence surprised him. Ty glanced up and stared. Bri's face was frozen in a mask of blanched whiteness. Her blunt fingernails were blue from clenching Cristine's shovel.

"Briony?"

"I won't ever be a mother." Her voice was icy.

That didn't make sense. She was great with Cristine. Ty ignored the warning note in her voice. "Why not? You'll meet someone. Fall in love. Have kids."

"No." She shook her head. "I have my work. That's enough."

"Are you kidding?" He frowned at her. "Work doesn't compensate for love. Not ever."

"I'm not saying it does. I'm simply saying that God has other plans for me. I've come to terms with that."

Ty watched the pain sift across her face and wanted to know why she was so ready to give up on a family. He itched to ask her about her past. But he didn't dare. Something in her expression, some dark specter at the back of her eyes warned him that Briony Green didn't allow anyone to see inside her heart, to the hurting part she kept locked away.

"Cristine does need a mother, though. Any thoughts in that direction?"

Ty grimaced, fully aware that she'd twisted the focus of the conversation away from herself and onto him.

"I was married once. I won't marry again. Cristine will be just fine."

He stared directly at Bri, daring her to ask any more on the subject. He'd respected her privacy. She would have to respect his.

"You must have loved Andrea a lot."

"Do you want a drink, honey?" Ty ignored the comment and turned his attention on Cristine. "Juice?"

She nodded, her hands clapping with joy. Ty swung her up into his arms and settled down on the quilt. He pulled out the juice and poured some into her sipping cup. Cristine grabbed on with both hands and sucked greedily.

Ty laughed at her. "You sound like a piglet."

"She goes into everything with gusto, doesn't she." Briony stood staring down at the little girl, a flicker of love shining in her eyes.

"Would you like some juice? I packed plenty. There's also a thermos of coffee, if you'd rather have that." He waited for her to sit down.

"I should have brought something along. I never even thought of it." She flushed with embarrassment at the oversight.

"We've plenty. Here—" he said, handing her a bottle of orange juice. He cuddled Cristine and began to gently rub her tummy, watching as her eyelids drooped. "She'll nod off pretty soon," he murmured. "The fresh air just zonks her out."

"I think it has more to do with your touch. She's a daddy's girl." Bri looked at the two of them. "You're the kind of father most kids dream of. She's fortunate."

"I'm trying." He liked knowing she approved. "If only I can stay her daddy, I'll be content."

"You don't want more children?" she asked, then hurried to cover her lapse. "I'm sorry, that was very rude."

"Cristine is the only child I'll ever have. I don't intend to lose her." Ty saw a shadow flicker through the blue eyes so like his daughter's. "Is something wrong?"

"Not wrong, really. But not right, either." She played with the baby's fluttering hand as she related her meeting from the evening before. "I'm afraid my investigations aren't progressing. I have no clue who Cristine's biological father is now that this Kent is out of the picture. I even went through the diary very quickly last night, looking for another name."

"Nothing?" His heart plummeted. "Not even a hint?"

She shook her head.

"Well, thanks for taking it this far." Ty almost wished she hadn't told him. With every step Briony took in her research, he felt less and less secure as Cristine's father, legal adoption papers notwithstanding.

"Oh, I'm not letting go completely. I still have a couple of other avenues I'd like to pursue while I'm here."

"Such as?"

Ty liked the way she sat there calmly, not panicked, not tense, as he was. Briony had a certain inner peace that seemed to settle like a cloak about her shoulders. It seemed she could weather any storm. Ty envied her that serenity.

"I'd like to talk to a few other people at the hotel. Maybe visit Sunshine."

"The ski hills are closed," he reminded her.

"I know, but there might be someone hanging around who knew Bridget, or this Kent Young." She sat quietly, hands folded in her lap, eyes pensive as they studied the sleeping child.

He shook his head, his fingers tightening around the baby. "I hate this! Why can't we just call up the lawyers and demand they open the file and tell us? Why do we have to pussyfoot around? It'll take forever!"

She stared at him, eyes wide with surprise.

"Sorry," he muttered, feeling the heat sting his cheeks as Cristine jerked awake. He soothed her, then apologized again.

"I didn't mean to yell. It just gets to me. I feel so helpless. My whole future rests right here," he muttered, staring down at Cristine. "How am I supposed to just sit and wait to see if someone pops up who will claim her?"

"I know it must be very difficult." Briony's soft hand covered one of his, just for a moment. "I'm sure you must wish I'd never come here, asking questions, probing into things."

"No." He shook his head, only then realizing that he was glad she'd persisted. "It's better to know up front than to have it sprung on you. Besides, I'd rather deal with this now, while Cristine's too young to understand, than later when she would experience the insecurity of not knowing where she belongs.''

Briony smiled, shook her head, then glanced down. ''I don't think Cristine will ever doubt where she belongs.''

''I hope not.'' He felt his heart pinch with love for the tiny bundle of joy he held. ''I guess I'd better get to it if I'm going to do some fishing.'' He lifted Cristine and settled her down in the playpen he'd placed next to the quilt. A soothing hand on her back stilled her fretful motions. Minutes later the mosquito netting was in place.

''Okay, Professor. Wanna learn how to fish?''

Her eyes expanded exponentially. ''Oh. I'm not actually—''

''Aw, come on, Briony. Live it up. Try something different for a change.''

''How do you know I don't try something different every day?''

''Yeah, right.'' He laughed. The prof? Take a risk? It was unthinkable.

Bri bent over, tying up her shoes as she spoke. ''Believe me, Tyrel, caring for Cristine is a life-altering experience every single day I'm with her.''

He chuckled. Now that he could believe. ''Then you're ready to branch out. Come on.''

''I have a feeling you're not going to give up on this.'' She sighed, nodded and lurched to her feet.

''Correct.'' He checked Cristine once more, then led the way to the edge of the water.

''Now, the first thing we do is hook on one of these little worms.''

She winced, but gamely forced the worm onto her hook.

Ty made fun of her. "The prof is squeamish? A scientist? Who knew?"

"I'm a botanist. I don't work with worms very much," she told him. "If I did, I'd change professions. These things are slimy."

"You did it! All right, now cast like this—" He demonstrated.

She cast. And snagged his shirt.

"Not quite." Ty freed himself, wincing as he tore the fabric. "Try again."

She did. This time she hooked his shoe.

"I don't think this is my forte," she muttered.

Ty considered her comment an extreme understatement. Still he persisted. For some reason it seemed important to him to show her she could do it. "Don't give up yet. Give it another try."

The third time, Briony finally struck the water— about two inches offshore. Water splashed up and caught him in the face. Frustration nipped at Ty's heels. He wanted to grab the rod from her hands, do it for her.

He wanted to get on with it.

Ah, yes. His mother's words tinkled in some distant cell of his brain. He choked down his impatience through sheer will.

"Good. Keep at it."

"The worm's gone." She peered at the end of her rod as if it consumed her attention. Her eyes switched to blink up at him in confusion. "What do I do with the fish when I catch it?"

Since there was a less-than-infinitesimal chance of her ever catching a fish, Ty snorted. He caught the downcast look on her face and quickly changed that to a cough.

"We'll take care of the fish when the time comes," he said. "Just keep practicing."

Ten minutes later Briony squealed her delight as the line flew across the water. The hook barely caused a ripple.

"I did it! I did it!"

"Wind it in," he yelled, envisioning his favorite red-and-white hook two hundred feet down in the glacial lake. "Slowly. That's too slow. Not that fast."

"Stop telling me what to do!" She glared at him.

Ty clamped his lips together and returned to his own pole, sneaking glances from the corner of his eye. She wound placidly for a few minutes. Then her face turned a ghastly pea green.

"Something's pulling back," she whispered.

"Just keep winding. Slowly." His own hook was so far out, he didn't dare stop to help. Instead, Ty tried to be encouraging. "Easy, just go nice and slow."

"I am going slo-o-w— Oh!" She yelped as the line ripped out, making a zipping sound.

"Don't drop it!" Why hadn't he given her the cheaper pole? That was his Father's Day gift from Cristine! Well, okay, so Ty had bought it himself, but still—

"It's coming in!"

Ty stared. Briony stood perched knee-deep in water, her clothes spattered by the scramble she'd made down the rock to catch the rod and reel she'd dropped.

"It's a fish," she squealed in a voice that was nothing like her usual solemn tone.

"That's what we keep in this lake, Briony. Fish. That's why it's called *fishing*." Ty, his own line finally secure, put down his pole and sauntered toward her, issuing directions as he went. "Just keep slowly winding. He'll tire out. No, don't lift it. Don't lift—"

Smack!

Seven pounds of cold, slimy fish caught him square in the mouth, slid down his shirt, then dropped to the ground. It was the biggest fish Ty had ever seen come out of these waters. And *she'd* caught it.

"Oh, my! Oh, mercy! What now? It's wiggling all over the ground, Ty. What do I do?" She was beside him now, dancing from one foot to the other as she stood guard over the pickerel she'd landed.

Ty picked up the fishing line, caught the fish by the gills and walked over to his tackle box.

"What are you doing?"

"Knocking it out. Then I'll put it on a stringer and—"

"Knocking it out? Don't you dare!" She stood in front of him, one hand on her hip, one finger wagging in front of his nose. "You're not going to hit my fish, Tyrel Demens. No way."

He stopped what he was doing and stared at her. "Well, how do you want to kill it, then?"

"Kill it? I'm not killing this poor defenseless animal!" She glared at him as if he were Jack the Ripper. "I hate animal abuse. I refuse to tolerate that kind of behavior, especially in a forest ranger." Her eyes clouded. "I thought you would be different."

"It's a fish, Bri! How do you think we eat the things if we don't kill them first?" Ty couldn't believe what he was hearing. She'd turned into a wild, illogical woman.

"Give me that!" She snatched the line out of his hands, marched back into the water and dropped the fish back in. It wiggled, mouth securely snagged on the hook.

"Oh, you poor thing. Move a little bit, that's it. You can get free if you try. You're not hurt, baby. Just try, okay. Just try." She crouched beside the water, encouraging all the while. When the fish didn't get free, she stepped right into the water and led it back and forth. "Go now. Go!"

"You'll kill it if you keep that up." He saw the pain in her eyes and gave up trying to figure out this woman. He also tossed any notion of fish for dinner.

"Give me the line. I'll release it."

"You won't hurt it?"

He clamped his lips together, tasted the fishy slime and grimaced. "No more than I have to," he promised.

After several soul-searching moments, she handed him the line. Ty quickly unhooked the fish, waggled it back and forth in the water, then glanced up at her. "You're sure?" he asked, hoping she'd change her mind.

"I'm sure. Let it go, Tyrel."

He let it go, staring mournfully after it. Then he walked back and stared at his own pole. Fishing had suddenly lost its allure. What Ty really wanted was a shower!

He glanced over at Bri and found her perched on top of the rocks, her shoes and socks laid out to dry. As he watched, she zipped off the bottom legs of her pants and laid them beside her shoes. Her long legs, perfectly visible in the blue shorts, were stretched out on the rocks, soaking up the sun.

"That was fun, wasn't it." She chirped it out as if they'd just finished tea. Her face glowed. "I guess you were right. It is good to try new things now and then. What should I try next?''

Ty had several responses, none of which were remotely appropriate. Instead of answering her, he whipped off his hiking boots and socks and waded into the frigid lake, vigorously scrubbing to remove all signs of fish from his clothes.

Some time passed before he noticed that the sun had disappeared. Ty glanced up, saw the dark clouds pushing up over the mountains and groaned. With his luck he'd come out of the lake just in time to get rained on.

His fishing day was ruined, he stunk to high heaven, and he'd missed out on the catch of the season because that coolly logical scientist didn't want to hurt a fish!

The sharp rock cutting into his foot did nothing to improve Ty's temper.

What did I do wrong this time, God? An icy droplet smacked him in the face, his only answer.

Chapter Six

&

"I like these ideas of yours to broaden my horizons."

Bri pretended her lungs weren't burning as she puffed up the long steep hill to the Upper Hot Springs.

"I've seen more of Banff in two weeks than I'd ever have seen on my own. I've never been here before, though I once visited Miette in Jasper. Is it the same?"

"Our Upper Hot Springs are older. No major renovations have been done here for a long time." Ty pushed Cristine's stroller with no obvious exertion, the mid-June sun emphasizing his dark good looks. "I haven't been here with Cristine for several months."

"The water isn't too hot for her?"

"It isn't this year. We had so much precipitation with the heavy snow pack. Then all the rain caused a runoff that's affected the temperature in the pool. That doesn't happen often. Let's just hope we're here before the crowds. It can get a little tight."

Ty insisted on paying for this excursion. "After all, I might need help with Cristine."

He and Cristine went one way, while Bri went off to change in the women's dressing room. She bundled her hair on top of her head, hoping she wouldn't have to dry it. It took so long, and she hated the dampness on her neck.

As she lowered herself into the spring, the warm water slid up her body like a silken sheath, enfolding her in its mineral softness.

Half a dozen bathers lounged in the water, and most of those seemed content to bask on the sunny side where they could stare out over the spectacular valley below them. Bri joined them, closing her eyes as the sun's warmth compensated for the cool breeze off the snowy mountaintops—

"Isn't that cute?"

Bri opened her eyes and found everyone's attention fixed on the big bronzed man murmuring to a tiny child as he carried her down the stairs. Ty nestled his baby girl against his chest, her frilly pink suit magnifying the richness of his dark chest hair. All the while he murmured soothing words, Ty walked deeper and deeper, until Cristine was completely wet.

He was so gentle. So tender. What would it be like to be cared for like that? How proud you would feel, to walk beside a man who loved like that, who lavished such care and attention on a little girl.

Just for a moment Bri's heart longed for that companionship, ached to share in that tender look of love and concern he gave Cristine.

"I'm sorry, Briony. I guess I never really loved you. I just thought you'd make a good mother for the boy."

The words stabbed at her, reminding her of her one foray into love. What a disaster! The shame and embarrassment of falling for someone who didn't love her had been nothing compared to the indignity of canceling the wedding and knowing he was going to remarry his first wife.

All those years ago. And yet, her determination was the same today as it had been then. She would never be a stand-in mommy, never be an add-on to a family simply to fill an emptiness inside herself. Never again would she allow herself to be tricked by soft words or soothing kisses.

The simple truth was, Briony Green was not the kind of woman men married. God had given her a brain. It was up to her to use it.

"Bee." Cristine spotted Bri and held out her arms, her grin wide.

"Hi, sweetie." Bri took the baby from Ty, her hands brushing his. That simple contact sent the blood rushing to her cheeks, so Bri concentrated on the child and her kicking legs. "You like the water, don't you, Cristine? Me, too."

"So you did call her by that name." An old man beamed from his perch on the big cement mushroom in the center of the pool. "I always wondered if you would."

"I beg your pardon?" Bri stared at him blankly, then sought Ty's interested gaze. He shrugged.

"You don't remember me, do you? I'm not surprised. You've had a busy year." The older gentleman reached out a hand and brushed Cristine's shoulder. "She looks just like you, as I predicted. Beautiful mommies always have beautiful babies."

Ty's grasp on her arm held Bri immobile. She couldn't have moved, anyway.

This man had known Bridget, had talked to her about the baby she would be having. In that split second, Bri made her decision. For now, she'd play the part of her sister.

"I'm sorry, I don't remember you," she murmured, gently swishing Cristine back and forth in the warm water.

"I suppose I'm not very memorable compared to your husband." The old fellow winked at Bri and thrust out a hand to Ty. "Rick Vicker," he bellowed, pumping Ty's hand as if he were grinding an organ. "I met your missus some time ago when I was here soaking. Arthritis, don't you know?" He leaned close to Ty. "Always worst in the winter."

"I'm sorry." Ty raised his eyebrows at Bri, obviously begging for help.

"I am, too, but it comes and goes. Not much you can do, 'cept try to ease the pain." Rick shrugged. "I drive up for the weekend sometimes and just sit and soak. Always helps." He smiled at Briony. "This one used to come and soak to get out the kinks that baby caused. We got to be friends when I kept reminding her that babies don't like their mommies in hot water."

Cristine kicked and splashed water at Rick and Ty. Rick simply laughed.

"Before they're born they don't like it. Not that I needed to remind her." He shook his head, eyes fondly remembering the past. "Your lady took real good care of that baby, talked to it when she thought nobody was looking. She'd be in and out ten times, either warming up or cooling down." He grinned at Briony's bathing suit with male appreciation.

"I 'spect that's how you got rid of the baby fat, isn't it?"

Briony gulped. What was she supposed to say to that?

Apparently nothing. Rick simply kept on talking.

"My wife never did get rid of hers. Every kid she'd complain she kept ten pounds. We had six of them."

"Oh." Ty took Cristine back, leaving Bri free to talk with Mr. Vicker. Ty's eyes issued some kind of a warning Bri didn't understand. Rick was speaking.

"So you decided to keep her, eh? I'm glad. She's a little sweetie, this one. Too precious to give away. When was she born?"

"March first." Bri ignored Ty's frown. She intended to clear up the misunderstanding, but not until she'd found out everything she needed to. This opportunity was heaven sent, and she didn't intend to waste it.

"Is that a fact?" He scratched his bald head. "Why, that's the day after I last saw you. I remember 'cause the twenty-ninth of February is my birthday and coming here was the birthday present I gave myself."

"That was—"

"The other one didn't come that day, did she?" He frowned, trying to remember. "No, she wasn't here. I'd have remembered that bright red bathing suit of hers."

"Mr. Vicker, I think I should—"

"Say, you must be the young man she was waiting for back then!" Rick studied Ty from head to foot, his face less friendly now. "Don't know why I thought you were smaller. Fellows in the Forces aren't tiny little weasels."

The Armed Forces? Briony tucked that away.

"You should have married her before you left, young man. Never take a chance is my motto. Those peacekeeping missions sound safe, but you never really know when your time is up."

"No, I suppose you don't." Briony spoke for Ty, who seemed lost by the verbiage. "Mr. Vicker, I should apologize. I think the woman you're talking about is, was, my sister Bridget."

He frowned. "Was?"

Bri nodded. "She died not long ago. I only found out she'd had a baby after she died, and so I came to Banff to meet Cristine. This is Cristine's father, Tyrel Demens."

"I'm sorry to hear about that." Rick was silent only a moment. "She was a real nice girl. Your hair's longer than hers was," he announced. "Other than that, I can't see a whole lot of difference. Same eyes, same build."

"Well, we were twins."

"Humph!" Rick glared at Ty. "So when did you get back?"

"Get back?" Tyrel glanced up from trying to keep Cristine off the cement mushroom. "I, uh, didn't get back."

"Ty is Cristine's *adoptive* father, Mr. Vicker. We were hoping you might know something about her real father."

"Not the father?" The old man looked disgruntled, then pinned Ty with a frown. "Why didn't you just tell the truth up front?"

"I'm afraid that's my fault. I've been trying so hard to find out about my sister's life here that I thought it wouldn't hurt to let things slide. I hope you'll forgive me?"

"I guess. Though I don't like liars." He glanced sideways at Ty, then leaned nearer to Bri. "Always thought that fellow your sister got mixed up with was a liar. Air Force doesn't use bungee jumpers. Least-ways, not that I ever heard of.''

"You don't think her boyfriend was in the Air Force.'' Bri wished he would contradict her, but she didn't think it was likely judging by the scowl on the old man's face.

"I think he was a cheat and a liar. Never said it out loud, but I thought it all the same.'' His mouth tightened. "Just dumped her here, you know. She stayed, working every day, while he took off on some jaunt. Told her to wait, that he'd be back. Never came. Never even wrote.''

"Did you ever hear his name, Mr. Vicker?'' Bri held her breath and prayed harder than she ever had before.

"His name?'' Rick scratched his chin. "Don't rightly know. It was so long ago. She never talked about him much after that first time. We talked about the baby, though.''

Mr. Vicker explained how he'd come back to the pool periodically and met Bridget on several occasions. They'd even shared lunch a couple of times.

"Later on we didn't talk as much, not about that stuff. It seemed like she always had this woman with her. They'd laugh and talk. They were good together, chased the shadows away. Andrea, her name was. That's all I remember.''

Ty stopped playing with Cristine, his body stiffening. "Andrea?'' His voice barely carried above the voices of the group now entering the pool.

Bri moved closer to him, one hand covering his. "We already knew that,'' she reminded him.

Ty nodded. "I know what you said. It's just that—'' He swallowed; his shoulders jerked back.

Bri understood what he was going through. Ty clung to his conviction that she was wrong about Andrea, hoped she had confused his wife with someone else, some other woman. It was too painful to accept that the person he'd completely trusted had gone behind his back.

"Thank you very much for telling us all this, Mr. Vicker. We really appreciate it." Bri ordered her brain to think, to remember if there was some clue she'd missed. But her brain was too busy recognizing the effect Ty had on her.

She ached to hold him close, to comfort him, to offer some tiny crumb of hope that would wash away the confusion and bitter pill of deception. But Ty yanked his hand away from hers and turned his back on them.

"No problem at all." Rick studied Ty curiously. "I hope you find the information you need. Say, if I remember anything, how would I get in touch with you?"

Bri told him where to contact Ty, then watched Rick leave. Her glance flew to the big man with his precious child.

Please give me the right words that will help heal his hurt, Lord.

She gave him some time with Cristine, watching them surreptitiously as she swam back and forth across the deep end of the pool. His manner toward his daughter hadn't changed, but his eyes—black, hard—glittered with anger.

Briony couldn't let him deal with it alone.

"It doesn't really change anything, Ty. She gave you Cristine. She obviously wanted her as much as you did. What does it matter—"

"What does it matter?" He gritted his teeth, stemming the anger that simmered just below the surface. "My own wife lied to me. That matters."

"She just wanted a baby, Ty." Briony brushed her hand over Cristine's hair. "She just wanted a child."

"Do you think I don't know that? We were married for six years, Briony. After the first year, all Andrea talked about was a baby. I figured that much for myself." He held out Cristine. "Can you hold her for a minute while I get our towels? We can sit over there in the sun and dry off."

Bri took the baby and watched as he strode across the pool and up the steps. He returned minutes later with his ever-present video camera and some towels. He shot miles of footage of Bri with Cristine, then packed it away in a bag that he set in a dry corner.

By the time Bri fetched her own towel and claimed the lounge next to his, she knew they had to talk it out. At least some of it. He couldn't carry this burden for long.

She was thankful that the busload of Japanese tourists chatted loudly enough to drown out her words.

"You can tell me to butt out if you want to, Ty. And I will. But I really would like to understand."

He didn't yell at her, so Bri continued. "Why would Andrea have kept all this from you? Are you certain you didn't miss something she said? You admitted you were busy, tied up with a fire. Maybe she did tell you about Bridget and you brushed it off or something."

"I didn't brush anything off where Andrea was concerned." A muscle in his jaw flexed. He handed Cristine some beads. "I couldn't afford to."

"What does that mean?"

He sighed. "Andrea and I grew up in the same

neighborhood. She used to come to our place a lot. Her home life wasn't the best and it bothered her. She sometimes stayed with my parents while I attended college. Then we got married. I don't think she ever really recovered from the abuse she suffered at home.''

"I'm sorry."

"So was I. I tried everything I could think of, but despite the doctors and the medications, Andrea had very bad days when she wouldn't talk. All she wanted to do was sleep." He smiled as Cristine bopped him in the chest with her beads. "I thought I knew her, knew the best way to care for her. I thought our marriage was what God wanted."

"Maybe it was." She hated that look of self-castigation on his face.

"I'm beginning to think everything I ever believed about her was a mistake." He stared at the water. "When Cristine came, I thought God had relented, given her a bit of peace. She loved to sit and watch Cristine sleep."

"I guess most new moms do."

"And then she died. No warning. No notice. Cristine was six weeks old. Six weeks! We didn't have time to share her. Six weeks wasn't long enough to build a family." His face tightened into a rigid mask of control.

"I've asked myself what I did wrong, what mistake I made that God would dump me in a situation where I had to raise a child alone. And now it's worse. Not only do I not know if Cristine's father will show up at some point and try to claim her, but now I've discovered my wife deliberately lied to me."

The grief and anger spilled out in a wash that grabbed at Bri's heart. She prayed silently for a moment, opening her mind to God's leading, as she watched Ty lift his daughter up to look out over the parapet.

"You're speaking as if God is after you, as if He's punishing you." She spoke softly, willing him to listen.

"Funny." He tossed her a mocking smile. "That's exactly how it feels."

"But God isn't like that. He doesn't get His jollies from ruining your world." She could hardly believe he'd said it.

"Doesn't He?" Ty pointed out the snow-topped mountains, his face softening as Cristine clapped her approval.

"No, He doesn't." Bri touched his arm. "God doesn't make mistakes, Ty. He doesn't have to go back and fix up some oversight. He works everything together for good. Everything."

"I used to think like that. I used to believe that I understood what He wanted for my life. But I don't think that anymore. Now everything just seems like a big mess."

He stood suddenly, lifting Cristine to his shoulders, where her view of the valley was unobstructed by the wrought-iron railing.

"It doesn't matter what it looks like, Ty. All we have to know is that God has everything organized, and then we proceed from there."

"Maybe His will is clearer to you than it is to me." A short huff, then the angry words burst out. "Apparently I didn't even know my own wife, Briony! And how can I possibly understand God's will or follow some nebulous plan for the future when I don't even know if I'll be able to keep Cristine?"

Bri prayed nonstop as she listened, aching to help him. The Japanese tourists eventually filed out, still chattering as they climbed the stairs. Only five people remained in the pool. It was the opening she sought.

"Give me Cristine," Bri said determinedly. He frowned. "It's all right. Just give her to me."

He handed over the little girl.

"Want to go swim again, sweetie?" Cristine's arms and legs flapped madly as she tried to gallop toward the pool. "Okay, come on." Bri glanced at Ty. "You, too."

Back in the water, Cristine squealed with delight. A lifeguard handed them inflatable arm bands, and Bri slipped them on Cristine's chubby arms. Slowly, carefully, Bri released her hands, just for a moment, and let Cristine float on her own.

Bri regained her hold before Ty could grab his daughter.

"How do you know Cristine won't drown?" She watched his face work, the emotions fluttering across. Anger, frustration, fear, hurt. Longing.

"She will if you let her go for too long." He grated out his answer, voice gruff with emotion.

Bri shook her head. "No, she won't, Ty." She let go again, watching carefully as the child kicked her legs. "You're not going to drown, are you, sweetie?" She cuddled the little body close. "Wanna try again?"

Cristine shrieked with joy, fist pummeling the water, sending up a spray that caught her in the face. She blinked, then let out a howl of dismay. Ty snatched her away from Bri, snuggled her close and whispered comforting words as he brushed away the water.

"You see, she's well protected. Her daddy is right there watching all the time. The minute she gets into trouble, he'll help her. But he also wants her to try new things, to learn about all the wonderful things she could enjoy if she'd just take a chance.'' She waited for him to absorb the idea.

"So I'm supposed to think that God snatching Andrea away when we needed her most was a—what? A learning experience?'' He snorted his disgust.

"Ty, when Cristine was on her own in the water, did she notice what you or I were doing? Did she see the lifeguards change when their shift ended or hear that truck change gears?'' Bri shook her head. "She was focused on the water in her eyes. She didn't understand that the lifeguard had to change before she got too tired, or that the truck had to slow down in order to speed up. It's all in the focus.''

"So I should focus on the greater good?'' His eyes were penetrating. "A motherless child is for the greater good?''

Bri smiled, unable to take offense when the words were so obviously torn from his heart.

"A father who adores you more than anything in this world is a wonderful thing to give a child,'' she whispered. "Maybe someday she'll have another mother. But through Andrea's actions, for whatever reason, you learned a depth of love and commitment you'd never known before. And despite what you thought at the time, God *was* in control. He was and is right here. You just have to trust.''

Some of the bleakness drained out of his eyes. "Is it so easy for you to have faith, Briony? Are you so certain of your path in life?''

"I guess I am certain of my path—now. But it wasn't always that way.'' She debated whether to bare the whole truth, then decided that she'd poked and probed into his personal life, so he had the right to know about her. It was only fair.

"Trust is still an issue I deal with almost daily."

"I don't know what you mean," he said. Little by little Ty was teaching Cristine that she could float on her own.

Bri took a deep breath. "When I was working on my master's thesis, a new professor took over my supervision. He lived on the same scientific planet I did, we shared our work every day." Now for the hard part. "And he had a seven-year-old son that I adored. I was certain God had sent me a man and a child I could love. A family of my own. I devoted myself to them, took time from my studies to care for the child. We decided to get married."

He stared at her as if he couldn't imagine her married.

"Three days before the wedding Lance called me. I'd been speaking at another university and I'd barely arrived home. He couldn't wait to inform me that his ex-wife had returned and that they'd just been remarried." She gritted her teeth and forced out the humiliating words.

"Apparently, Lance decided I'd make a good wife not because he loved me, but because he thought I'd make his son a good mother. Now that the boy's real mother was back and willing to work things out, he realized he'd always loved her. There was no need for a stand-in."

"Ouch!" Ty made a face. "I don't suppose he had the good grace to move away and leave you in peace?"

Bri shook her head. "No, I did that. After I canceled the wedding, there were still a lot of bills. I had to get a job to pay them off and in the process I lost a year's worth of work.'' She swallowed hard, then admitted the truth.

''But the worst of the whole thing was facing the fact that God had never intended for me to be a mother to that wonderful little boy.''

''Oh, but—''

She shook her head, a grim smile tweaking her lips. ''No, Ty. You've never seen me in the lab, or you'd understand how impossible it really is. I forget everything, including meals, other people, appointments.''

''You could get an alarm clock or a timer.''

Bri laughed. ''That's just part of the problem. I hate a mess. I like everything organized, clean, precise. You've seen that for yourself. How do you think a child would grow up with a mother like that?''

It hurt to say it, but as Briony had learned, the truth was a painful beast.

''You're very good with Cristine!''

His frown eased some of her heart-hurt. ''Only as a substitute, a temporary stand-in.'' No matter how tempting, Bri couldn't, wouldn't ever allow herself to imagine she could be more than that. As it was, leaving Cristine was going to be so hard.

She laughed as Cristine splashed again, spraying water over both of them. The gloom lifted.

''How did we get on this maudlin topic, anyway?''

He raised one eyebrow. ''As I recall, you brought it up to explain faith and trust. I don't think you can call it trusting God just because you don't want to get hurt again. The guy was a flake. There are others.''

''You misunderstood.'' Okay, she'd go through this once more, then it was history. ''The trust part came because I didn't give God enough credit, I didn't let

Him handle things. I grabbed on to Lance because I wanted his son, because I thought I would miss out on that experience.''

''Huh?''

''I substituted real love for like-mindedness between two people with compatibility, Ty. I thought his son was the bond that would keep us together. God knew it wouldn't. I had to learn that a stand-in mommy is no substitute for real love.''

Ty played with Cristine for several minutes, whooshing her back and forth. Finally he spoke, his voice devoid of emotion.

''She's tired. Shall we go?''

''Okay.''

But later, as they trundled down the street to the pizza place Ty loved, Bri wondered if she'd helped him at all.

''What I was trying to say back there was that Andrea's friendship with Bridget may have been God's hand, leading them to find comfort and solace with each other. And from that friendship came Cristine. *All things work together for those who love God.* All things, Ty. You've just got to have faith.''

''Maybe that's enough for you. But I'm not going to stop asking for answers.'' He guided them into the restaurant, his hand firm on her back. ''I need to know why my wife was so secretive. What was she hiding from me?''

Chapter Seven

❧

"I'm sorry, Bri. I just can't make it back in time to get to the gondola rides by six. Can we reschedule?" Ty dragged a hand through his hair, turning his back on the interested stares from the other rangers. "What about Friday?"

"Someone told me recently that I should stop being so tied to a schedule." Briony's voice brimmed with laughter. "I'm trying to take his advice."

"I meant it in the nicest possible way," he muttered, ashamed of his quick temper.

"I know. Actually, I'm, uh, busy with something here. Let's just see how things go, okay? There's no hurry to go on the gondola. No hurry at all. Do whatever you need to at work, Ty. We'll manage. Bye."

She sounded distracted, and Ty was pretty sure he knew the reason why. Briony had decided to get to the bottom of Bridget's mystery before she left town in thirteen days.

If he closed his eyes, Ty could imagine her sitting in his kitchen, glasses perched on the end of her nose as she analyzed the diary in minute detail. He wondered if she'd even remember he'd called.

"New lady in your life giving you a hard time, Tyrel?" His buddies harangued him constantly these days, especially since they'd seen Briony hiking with him and Cristine one evening last week. Briony had been collecting samples for her Calgary lab.

"Wish my wife would give me a hard time like that." The chief ranger batted his eyes, his voice hitting a wobbly falsetto. *"I'll take Cristine home if you'd rather do something else, Ty."*

"Yeah, Darlene's always nagging me to get home on time. If it isn't that, then it's the garbage or the kids. She never tells me to just take off and have fun."

Ty laughed. "But Darlene's a first-rate cook. That cake she sent over yesterday was a killer. Mmm."

The other rangers agreed, then fell to discussing their own families. As he listened, the bee of envy buzzed in Ty's mind. They grumbled a lot, but there wasn't one of his co-workers who'd willingly change places with Ty. They had the kind of marriage his parents had shared. Joy, anger, pride—they all flowed together, creating a loving unity.

He'd never had that with Andrea. From the beginning he'd known their marriage was about getting her away from her parents and the horror of her home life. He never doubted she loved him, not then and not now. What he'd begun to question were his own choices.

What made him think he could help her? Why had he been so certain that was the only way?

He'd prayed, that's why. Constantly. He'd believed God would get them through anything as long as they trusted.

The chief called the meeting to order and launched into a list of priorities. After the first five minutes, Ty fell into his own thoughts.

It was his fault Andrea's depression had worsened. All the classic signs were there, everything he'd been warned about. But he'd chosen to ignore her manic talk about babies, the pictures, the magazines, the books she collected in huge stacks.

Ty's skin crawled as he remembered their last trip to the fertility clinic—the day his dream had died.

He'd hated the place, hated the indignity of it, the aura of frenzy that clung to the very air. He'd hated the quiet desperation of the couples huddled in the waiting room, hope shining in their eyes, had shuddered at the disappointment that followed as they trudged away.

He'd gone through it twice. But the cost of the trips, the days off, the evaluations and medical procedures—all took their toll. In a way he'd been glad when Andrea finally agreed they weren't going back. Of course he'd felt sad at the pain teeming in her eyes, but inside relief reigned.

And then the sledgehammer felled him—he would never be a father. Adoption was their only recourse.

Tough weeks of intense heavenly questioning followed. Gradually, though, they'd found new promise in the Bible. Ty told himself he'd accepted God's will. Andrea worked herself out of the slump, concentrated on her therapist's instructions. They'd filled out form after form, hoping, always hoping. Five long years of waiting—for nothing.

"Ty, you can handle that, can't you?"

He blinked up at the chief, saw the pity in the other

man's eyes and knew he understood that Ty had been
focused on the past.

"I mean, you don't have to actually climb Castle
Mountain. We know that little girl of yours keeps you
climbing enough." They all laughed. "Anyway, the
tree line doesn't go very high and the bears won't be
hard to track, if they've moved that far."

Ty caught on immediately. Bear checks. He nodded.
"Sure, no problem. Anything else?"

"Yeah. It's your turn to bring the goodies for coffee
time. That does *not* mean we want you to bake."

They spent a good ten minutes teasing him about
the state of his brownies. By the time he was leaving,
the sun and surrounding mountains were completely
obliterated by a thick heavy mist.

Ty walked out, then stuck his head back inside the
door. "Hey, Chief. If it pours tonight, that footbridge
over by Maligne Lake is going to be washed out.
There's a group of hikers scheduled to go through
there over the weekend."

His boss nodded. "Thanks. Almost forgot your report on that. I'll get someone to check it out. You head
on home now."

Ty nodded and left, his eyes automatically scanning
the parking lot and surrounding streets for unpredict-
able elk. The herds were fond of roaming the town for
food whenever they pleased. Ty had no intention of
surprising a cow and her calf enjoying a late-evening
lunch beside his Jeep.

All clear.

He drove toward home, planning to stop by the tiny
bakery ahead. Unfortunately, it was closed, and he'd
have to come up with some other idea for the guys'
snacks.

At home, Bri and Cristine lay sprawled on the floor in the living room, the fire crackling behind them. If ever Ty had visualized a homey scene, this was it. Blond heads snuggled together, they were studying the animal book Cristine loved.

Both females looked up at the same time, smiles mushrooming across their faces until two sets of vivid blue eyes glowed. The problems of the day evaporated. He was home.

Cristine was the first to move. She wiggled herself upright and tumbled headlong toward him. "Da!" she screamed at the top of her lungs.

Ty stared at her in delight. He gathered her plump little body into his arms and hugged tightly. His eyes met Briony's.

"She said 'Dad,'" he whispered, emotion welling up inside.

Bri nodded, eyes shining with pleasure. "She's been practicing all day. I videotaped her. I noticed you've been doing it quite a lot. I hope you don't mind."

Mind? He wanted to hug her for thinking of it. Cristine was his only chance at fatherhood. Ty intended to record every second of her childhood. Then, when he was old and alone, he'd watch it and be warmed by the memories.

"No. I don't mind." He shook his head stupidly. "Not at all. Thank you."

"Da. Da. Bee."

"She's building quite a vocabulary."

Bri's voice was quiet. Too quiet. Ty frowned. There was something about her eyes. He felt a shiver of apprehension.

"What happened?"

She gathered herself up and perched precisely on

the edge of the sofa, her feet together, hands clasped primly in her lap.

"I did something you may not approve of," she told him, eyes meeting his without pause. "I ran an ad in several newspapers asking anyone who knew Bridget to contact me."

"Contact you? Here?" Ty couldn't believe she'd done it. This was asking for trouble, bringing it right to his door.

Bri's shoulders lifted as she deflected his questions. "No, I used my former address and had all mail forwarded to me here. I received a response today."

He forced himself to sit because there was nowhere else to go. You couldn't run away from pain, escape the hurt that God meted out. Whatever justice He demanded had to be done.

Ty set down his squirming daughter. He took a deep breath. "Go on."

"There is a woman who worked with Bridget. She lives in Vancouver now, but two-and-a-half years ago she was working in Reservations at the Banff Springs Hotel."

"That's where your sister was employed." The words came out in a dull, flat voice that he had no control over. Ty waited for the ax to fall.

"Apparently Bridget trained her." She glanced once at Cristine, checking, then focused on him. "Are you all right?"

"I'm fine." That was a lie. He wasn't fine. He was more afraid than he'd ever been in his life. One advertisement, and Briony Green could tear apart his life. "Go on," he said through clenched teeth, handing Cristine the small doll she'd dropped.

Bri scrutinized him before she continued. "Apparently Bridget knew this woman for several months. They talked a lot about their lives.''

''Her name?''

''Isabelle. Isabelle Edwards.'' She quirked an eyebrow. ''Does it mean something?''

Ty shook his head.

''Oh. All right. Well, then.'' She took a deep breath.

''Briony, get to the point, will you? I don't care about all the details. I don't need to know every single word she wrote.'' He held on to his temper by a thread. ''I hate all this preamble. Just tell me what this woman had to say!''

''I wasn't deliberately—''

Ty glared at her, white-hot fury dancing through his veins.

''She knew Bridget's boyfriend. They double-dated a few times.'' She spilled it out in a rush of words. ''Peter Grant. The name of Bridget's boyfriend is Peter Grant.''

''And does this know-it-all woman have any idea where we might find Mr. Peter Grant?'' He crossed his arms over his puffed-out chest. ''Well?''

''She thinks he had his own business, but at the time she knew Bridget, Peter worked for a bank in Calgary.'' Briony licked her lips, her face flushed.

She hated being pushed like this, he knew, hated the disruption in her logical presentation. But Ty couldn't stop the words. Every cell in his body urged him to snatch up Cristine and run as far and as fast as he could, away from the threat, away from the danger of losing his child.

''I took the liberty of calling the head offices of several banks. Peter Grant worked in the downtown branch of the Bank of Montreal, but he's no longer employed there.'' Bri lifted her head, her eyes brimming with tears. "I'm sorry, Ty. So sorry."

"I'm not.'' He felt a bitter glee well up inside. "I wish he were gone for good. I wish no one could ever find him.'' He saw her stare and shrugged. "I know it's not the right thing to say. But that's the way I feel."

"But he may not know about Cristine," she reasoned.

"Get real! If this *boyfriend* saw Bridget even eighteen months ago, he could hardly miss the fact that she was pregnant. It's obvious he didn't want the responsibility so he just walked away."

Suddenly Ty was sick of it, sick of the whole mixed-up, confusing mess. He wanted it settled. Now. Before he lost more time.

"I'm taking tomorrow off. I'm going to Calgary." The minute he said it, he knew it was the right thing.

"To do what? I told you, Peter is no longer at the bank."

"But someone there may know where he is, what he does, how to contact him. I intend to get to the bottom of this.'' He surged to his feet. The decision lifted an enormous weight off his shoulders. For now.

"While I'm there, I intend to check with my lawyer. Perhaps he'll have some suggestions.'' He dared her to argue.

"I did phone the lawyers that were named on the adoption certificate,'' she murmured. "They don't seem to have any information on Peter."

"Then, they can find some. If it's there, I intend to know about it.'' He swung Cristine up into his arms and hugged her close. "Daddy's not letting you go, sweetie. Not ever,'' he whispered, brushing her downy head against his cheek.

He felt Bri's hand on his arm.

''I wasn't trying to hurt you.'' Tears clumped her lashes together, poised to fall from the corners of her gorgeous eyes. ''I was trying to help. I want you to keep Cristine always. I know how much you love her.''

Ty lifted an arm and hugged her close against his side. She smelled like baby powder and lemons and just a hint of spice. And she fit into his arm as if she were made to be there.

''I wasn't blaming you,'' he murmured, watching as Cristine played with Briony's braid. ''It's just that—''

''You're an action man. You've got to be up and doing while I like to mull everything over.'' She nodded, her smile misty. ''I know. I tend to think that my way is the only way there is. I forget that there are other ways.''

Ty stared down into her eyes—eyes filled with compassion and caring. She was so generous, so sensitive. He'd have to tread carefully. Ty set Cristine down, watched for a moment as the little girl settled in to play with her blocks. Then he turned back to Briony.

''I haven't got your patience, Bri. I've spent too many hours wondering when the ax would fall, when something would happen to ruin what I've got. I can't live that way anymore.''

''Don't say that!'' She brushed her hand over his chest. ''Why should you be afraid? You believe in God, you know He's going to do what's best.''

Ty had to smile. She was so naive, so trusting. It hurt him to shatter her illusions, but she didn't realize the ramifications of Peter Grant's existence. He did.

Ty cupped her cheek in his hand, his thumb brushing over her jawline.

"Briony, you've got your beliefs, and I respect that. But I'm not sure God and I agree on what's best for Cristine." He spoke frankly. "I told you, I don't understand His ways. I don't have the faith you do."

Her eyes widened. "But you could have," she whispered.

He shook his head. "No. I can't. Not anymore."

She studied him, puzzled. "Why?"

"Because I think I hate Him." There, it was out. Sheer relief to have finally said it.

"Oh, Ty, you don't hate God. God is love." She looped her arms around his waist and leaned her head on his chest, exhibiting the trust she spoke of.

Ty drew away, just enough so he could look straight at her.

"He took everything, Bri. My hopes for a family, my future with Andrea. Now Cristine is threatened. I can't just sit back and wait for it to happen. Do you understand? I have to do something."

"You're going to fight God?" A tender smile fluttered over her lips. "You're taking on the Almighty Builder of the Universe because you don't like the way He's handling things?" She shook her head, her expression full of mirth. "Sounds like pretty poor odds to me."

He would have drawn away then, would have reverted to acting like a boss would, but she wouldn't allow it. She kept her arms in place, wrapped tightly around his waist, her eyes focused on his face.

"He doesn't want to hurt you, Ty." Her voice wove over him like a web of calm. "He wants the best for you. He aches to give you the delights of your heart.

He loves you far more than you can even imagine.'' She leaned back, just a little, her face shining with joy.

"How much love can you imagine, Ty? A couple getting married, a new baby born, sharing a birthday with your best friend? What?'' Her eyes dared him to answer. "Go ahead, try.''

"I don't know,'' he muttered at last, irritated by her dog-with-a-bone persistence.

"Think of Andrea and of how much you loved her,'' she murmured, head tilted to one side. Then her gaze swept to the carpet. "Now, think of Cristine. Yes, I can see your love for her. It blazes in your eyes. Can you feel it here?'' Her palm covered his heart. "Can you feel the warmth of that love spilling through you, touching everything with a bright glow?''

The beauty and wonder of her words caught him in a spell, weaving the fantasy around him with silken threads.

"How much will you love her when she starts school? Tries out for basketball? Starts ballet classes? Won't that love grow and deepen even more?''

He nodded, the pictures building, gaining momentum in his brain.

"And when you walk her down the aisle on her wedding day, won't your heart be full to bursting with love for her?'' Bri brushed back his hair, her eyes glistening as she nodded. "Yes, it will. But even then, Ty, even then at that most special moment, you won't feel the tiniest fraction of the love God feels for you right now.''

"Then why, Briony?'' he whispered, pressing his cheek against her hair as he tried to comprehend. "If He loves me that much, why must I go through all this pain and heartache?''

She hugged him close. "I don't know, Ty. I simply don't know. I'm certain of only one thing. Nothing can separate us from the love of God—"

The words came faintly to his ear, muffled by his shirt.

"If you ask me, that's a pretty powerful love."

Ty held her for a long time, savoring the strength and comfort he found in her presence. It surprised him that she fit so perfectly—not just into his arms, but into his life.

She drove him crazy, of course. Her perfectionist attention to details, her nitpicky insistence on order and organization, her constant analyzation of every option made him nuts.

But he couldn't fault her dedication to Cristine or her unwavering commitment to finding the truth, no matter what. Her staunch determination to do the right thing, to be sure her sister's child was well cared for, touched him.

Briony Green might be meticulously organized and efficient to the point of tediousness, but she had a quiet loving heart that was unstinting when it came to caring for someone else.

She deserves to have a family, God. She deserves a chance to be a mother to her own child. She has such a capacity for love when she lets herself go.

She'd be a wonderful wife.

The thought came from nowhere, blindsiding him. When had he started thinking of Briony as anything other than Cristine's caregiver?

Ty stood with her head resting on his shoulder and asked himself what had prompted him to see Bri in this new light. Was it her understated beauty? The quiet way she waited for him to speak first? Or was it her faith and assurance that God would do exactly as He'd promised?

When had this attraction built into something stronger, something he dearly wanted to explore? She had brought calm and peace to his life in just a few short weeks, made him believe there was still a chance for happiness.

Marry again?

The idea barely popped into his mind before he tossed it. It could never be. It was impossible. God had taken Andrea because He wanted Ty to manage alone. Very well, he'd manage. Alone. On his own. If he lost Cristine, he'd handle that, too. But he couldn't, wouldn't make the mistake of involving anyone else in his pain. Not again.

Carefully, he moved his hands, wrapping his fingers around Bri's arms as he edged away. Ty avoided her eyes, detoured around her to pick up Cristine.

"I'm going to Calgary tomorrow," he said, pretending nothing had happened. "I'm going to check out Mr. Peter Grant. If there's a clue to unravel this, I intend to find it." He glanced up, saw the confusion cloud her eyes, and softened just for a moment.

"I have to know, Briony. I have to get answers."

"You may not find them," she reminded him.

"Then, at least I'll have tried. Sitting here, waiting for God to respond, hoping He'll send down something from heaven—it just isn't working."

He sank into the armchair, cuddling Cristine against his chest. The little girl snuggled close, her eyelashes drooping with tiredness.

"I've got to do everything I can. Everything," he said.

Bri walked across the room picking up toys,

straightening things, until she'd made her way in front of his chair. She studied him for several moments, then nodded.

"Yes, I can understand that. I'd like to go with you."

Ty frowned. He'd expected to handle it alone.

"I want to know as badly as you do, Ty. Besides, I promised Bio-Tek that I'd stop in their office and fill out some paperwork before I start my new job." She bent to brush her lips over Cristine's head. Her eyes met his. "We could stop by your sister's so your mother could see Cristine. She's phoned almost every day. I think she's lonely."

Ty considered it for a moment. "Okay. We'll leave at eight-thirty." He watched as Bri gathered up her ever-present briefcase.

"You're a fraud, Dr. Green," he murmured, never stopping in his rhythmic caress of Cristine's back. "You'd like everyone to think you're a cool, dispassionate scientist who's only interested in the facts."

She stopped what she was doing to stare at him. "But that's exactly who I am!"

Ty shook his head, eyes twinkling at her confusion. "Uh-uh. Deep inside that busy brain you're a marshmallow, Prof. You go out of your way to help, from taking on a child you've never met, to looking for your sister's boyfriend, to meeting my sister. You just can't help it, can you?"

Her cheeks blushed red. Bri turned so that her back was to him as she repacked her lists and charts.

"I don't know what you're talking about. I just happen to want things neatly tied up before I leave, that's all."

Leave. Ty mentally winced. How could he have forgotten? He'd been acting as if Briony would be around forever, and she had less than two weeks left. The thought hurt on some level he didn't even understand.

Alone again.

"Ty?" She stood at the door, umbrella in hand, waiting for his response.

"Yeah?"

"You're okay? There's nothing more I can do?"

He shook his head. "I'm fine. Thanks. I'll see you in the morning. We'll pick you up."

She hesitated, then nodded. "All right. Good night."

Ty glanced up just long enough to see the questions fill her face. His eyes met hers, locked and held, as the memory of that embrace simmered in the air. If only...

"Good night, Briony," he whispered.

She was already gone.

He was alone. As God intended.

"But I've still got Cristine," he whispered. For once, Ty found no assurance in his own words.

Chapter Eight

"I'd rather be arriving than leaving Banff." Briony glanced over her shoulder at the receding mountains and sighed. "It's going to be hard to leave, to go back to the city."

Ty checked on Cristine in his rearview mirror, then gave Bri a mocking smile. "Ah, but you'll be in your lab, Dr. Green. Oblivious to the world."

She thought about that for a moment. It sounded deathly dull compared to her time with Cristine. "I suppose" was all she said.

"Where do you think we should start?" he asked, passing several RVs as they rolled down the highway through the foothills. "At the bank?"

Bri shook her head. "No, actually I thought it might be better to stop at Bio-Tek first. They're on the far side of the city. We'll work our way back from there." She tugged out her city map and a pencil. "What's your sister's address again?"

Ty told her. She eventually found it on the map and noted it with a bright red marker.

"Yes, you see if we work our way across the city we can end up near her house and not have to backtrack." She smiled at the simplicity of it.

"I might have known you'd say that. Always organized." He glanced at the briefcase. "What else do you have in there?"

Her cheeks betrayed her, burning bright with embarrassment. "Just a list of a few questions I thought we might ask. Also, perhaps we could check the hospital where Cristine was born, see if they remember anything."

"That's a long shot."

"I know. But long shots are all we seem to have." She wished it weren't so. If only Bridget had told her *something,* confided in her before she died. "I read some more of the diary last night."

"Oh." His eyes narrowed. "Anything?"

"Well, nothing specific, perhaps. But I feel the tone of her writing changes at one point. She's talking about work, about the baby. She seems excited. It sounds as if she intends to raise Cristine herself. It's hard to read dates—to know if she means day, month, year or month, day, year—but apparently a week passes."

"And?" Impatient as usual, Ty's fingers gripped the wheel. "What does she say then?"

"She talks mostly about making sure 'the baby' has a good home."

"'The baby'?" He frowned. "Why do you say it like that?"

"Because up to then it was 'my baby.'"

Ty's words brimmed with kindness. "This is hard for you, isn't it?" He rolled his eyes. "Now, that was a stupid question."

"Yes," Bri agreed after a moment's thought, "it is

hard sometimes. My parents would have loved Cristine.''

''Would have?'' He frowned.

''They died several weeks after Bridget. A car accident.''

His hand covered hers, squeezed, then continued to hold it on the leather seat separating them.

''I'm very sorry, Briony. You've had a really tough time.''

''Thanks.'' She sat and absorbed the comfort he offered, content to accept it without feeling guilty.

Though at first she'd thought Ty unemotional and harsh with everything except his daughter, she'd come to appreciate that this man possessed a wonderful ability to empathize. He had no patience with tales of woe, but when someone mattered to Ty, he was fiercely protective. She'd seen pictures of Andrea wrapped tightly in his arms, as if he could protect her from the world.

What would it be like to be loved like that? To know that someone would tackle anything to keep you safe, that they loved you that much? It was Bri's secret fantasy to be loved like that. An aching little dream she kept tucked away inside, where no one could see that the scientist was a dreamer.

Ty, of course, wouldn't believe it. To him she was Cristine's caretaker, a necessary nuisance whose oddball foibles had to be tolerated for exactly thirty days, until his mother returned. He probably assumed that his life would return to normal after that.

But Mrs. Demens's return was not at all assured. Bri knew she'd be better able to assess the situation today, when they stopped by. Perhaps she'd also be able to persuade Ty's sister to help her come up with some other scenario. If Bri found Cristine a taxing responsibility, what would she be like for Mrs. Demens?

"What are you thinking about?" He turned as indicated and followed the Crowfoot Trail. "You've been quiet most of the way. Like someone else."

Bri glanced back, smiling at Cristine's sleeping face. "Actually I was thinking about you," she admitted, surprising herself.

"Me? That's pretty boring."

"I was wondering if you'd ever had to rely on someone else."

He frowned, his eyes full of questions. "I suppose we all rely on others to some extent."

"That isn't exactly what I meant." Bri thought for a moment, rewording it in her mind. "Have you ever been in a situation where you've had to let go and just trust that someone else would do the best they could for you?"

He shook his head once, decisively. "I've usually managed pretty well on my own steam. I get a fix on the problem and then find a solution."

It sounded so simple. Briony had to smile.

"So you just set your goals and go for it?"

He nodded.

"What happens when it doesn't work out?"

He pulled up in front of Bio-Tek, then gave her an odd look. "Why are you asking me this?"

"I'm a little concerned about today," she admitted. "There's no guarantee that we'll find anything that will help us. What are you going to do if it turns out this was a dead end?"

It was obvious such a thought had never even entered Ty's realm of thinking. He puzzled over it for a moment, then shrugged.

"Reevaluate and form a new plan," he replied. Then he climbed out of the truck to free Cristine.

"Oh, boy! Move-or-get-out-of-the-way Tyrel Demens is in charge." Briony unclasped her seat belt as she whispered a prayer for help. "But what if you can't change it," she insisted, walking beside him toward the sprawling white complex. "What if there's not a single, solitary thing you can do to change what God's given you?"

Ty jerked to a stop, his mouth tight, lips pinched. His eyes chilled Briony as they glared into hers.

"Then you deal with it and move on to something else. Any other questions?" He jiggled Cristine, hushing her complaints. "Look, you don't have to give us a tour of Bio-Tek today if you don't want. Maybe some other time would be better."

Hurt pinched her heart. Bri pretended it didn't matter.

"If you don't want to waste time today, it's perfectly all right with me," she murmured, tugging open the solid glass door. "I'll try not to hold you up."

"Briony." His hand came out to stop her hurried pace toward the receptionist, his fingers squeezing her arm. "I truly didn't mean to say it like that. Cristine and I would love to see everything. I guess your questions just got to me."

"Why?" She simply stood, waiting.

He hesitated, his eyes on the floor. "There's only been one time in my life when I've faced a situation I desperately wanted to change and couldn't. I don't much like talking about it." His lips clamped together like a clam about to spill the pearl.

It was probably rude, but Bri asked, anyway. "Why not?"

His fingers tightened on her arm. But Ty didn't even seem to notice. As she watched, he hugged his daughter closer. His eyes softened, melted, an overwhelming pain washing through them as he gazed down at Cristine.

"Because it hurts," he admitted at last, his voice a whisper of regret. "It still hurts, Bri. And probably always will."

"I'm sorry." Bri yearned to know what cut through his implacable assurance to wound so deeply. She wanted to offer—what? Something to make it go away?

"Thank you." The moment stretched between them. Their gazes caught, held. His hand relaxed, his fingers brushing the skin he'd clutched.

"I wasn't just probing, you know," she said, conscious that all around them people were watching. "I was trying to prepare you for today, for the disappointment."

"I'll be fine. But thank you. Again." He lifted his hand away and brushed it against her cheek, fingers sliding over the skin, past her jaw and down her neck.

"Miss Green? How wonderful to see you here today. And you've brought the little girl! She's delightful." Her future boss stood beside them, waiting to be introduced.

"Dr. Natelle, I didn't expect you to stop your work just to show us around." Bri introduced Ty and Cristine, but remembering Ty's wish to hurry she didn't offer any explanations.

The doctor insisted on a full tour, pointing out Bri's office and her portion of the lab, and then spreading out a map outlined in dark blue, the area of Banff National Park where she'd be collecting samples.

"All of the collection has to be done first, of course. Then we'll begin testing to see which strains we can alter enough to withstand the bugs."

After three-quarters of an hour, Briony insisted they had to go.

"As long as you're staying in Banff, you might want to scout out a place to live while you do your fieldwork." Dr. Natelle tapped the end of his nose with his pencil. "The summer months are often busy, and I'd hate to see you stuck in limbo, Miss Green. After all, your real work can't begin until the samples are collected and tested."

A minute later the doctor's assistant carried him off with news of a problem in the lab, leaving Ty and Bri to exit the building without fanfare.

"So you'll be coming back to Banff," Ty murmured, fastening Cristine back into her car seat. "I didn't realize that."

"I expect it will take some time before the actual genetic altering takes place. Of course, it would be simpler if they'd set up a temporary lab in Banff, but the doctor wants everything in-house. Makes for a lot of traveling." She waited for Ty to close her door and climb in the other side.

"Okay, bank first?" she asked, after he'd started the truck.

Ty shrugged. "I guess. We have to start somewhere. Which way?"

They tried three branches before they found someone who actually remembered Peter Grant.

"Oh, Peter. Sure. He hasn't been here for a while, though." The bank clerk shrugged. "He was only temporary."

Ty tossed an I-told-you-so look at Bri.

"What did you want to know?" The woman admired Cristine, her eyes soft. "Your little girl is so cute. She looks like her mom."

"Yes, she does." Bri smiled, thinking of Bridget. "Actually we'd like to know anything you can tell us."

"Okay." She thought for a moment. "Peter was an extreme type. You know, on the edge."

Ty frowned. "I don't think I do know. Can you elaborate?"

"Eight-hour jogs, bicycling Borneo, that kind of thing. When he was here, he was planning some sheer-face mountain climbing. I forget what he called it."

"Rappelling?"

Ty's intensity bothered Bri. He was scaring their only contact.

The woman took a step back, her face wary as she sputtered a half laugh.

"Well, it was repelling to me, that's for sure. Letting yourself fall down the edge of a mountain?" She shook her head. "Not my idea of a good time."

"Mine, either." Bri stepped in. "Did he tell you where he was going to do this? Or when?"

"He was in training, I remember that much. He spent his lunch hours at that new gym around the corner. Claimed he had to get in shape for some eco-challenge he wanted to enter." The teller rolled her eyes. "I should be as out of shape as him."

"He was good-looking?" Bri took the baby from Ty and leaned closer to hear the answer. "All muscles?" Bridget had always preferred fit men, and edgy men.

"Yes, but not bulky. He was a little taller than me. Lean, sleek looking." She laughed. "Peter always reminded me of a panther. That honed muscular look, I guess. The blond hair didn't hurt any, not with that tan."

Ty, clearly impatient with this physical assessment, interrupted. "Do you remember when he last worked here? Or where he was going when he finished?"

"Let's see. It was summer, I think." She considered for a minute. "Yes, during summer vacation. I remember because Peter worked extra hours so some of the others could extend their leave."

"And then what did he do?"

"Hmm, good question." She tapped her lip. "After that, I'm pretty sure it was heli-skiing on Shuswap Lake. Or maybe the rappelling thing." She shrugged. "Sorry, but that's the best I can do after so long."

Bri saw her eyes move to the clock.

"You've been wonderful. Thanks so much for talking to us." But as the woman turned to leave, Bri asked her most pressing question. "Did you ever see him again? Hear from him or of him?"

"No. Sorry. He's probably in South America somewhere, though. Peter lived for a challenge."

"You don't happen to know if he had a girlfriend." Bri held her breath.

The teller nodded. "Yeah, now that you mention it, he did talk about someone. I never knew her name, just that she liked the same stuff he did. She must have lived in the mountains because they hiked together a lot." She glanced at the manager. "Look, I've really got to get back to work."

"We understand. Thanks a lot for speaking to us."

"I hope it helped." She tweaked Cristine's cheek. "Bye, honey."

Bri linked her arm through Ty's and walked him out

of the bank. He stopped, refusing to budge one more step, the moment they cleared the door. His chin jutted out in grim determination.

"I had more questions, you know." His eyes flashed his anger. "Maybe you asked all you needed to, but—"

"We couldn't hold her any longer, Ty. She'd already done us a favor by talking to us. Besides, what else could we have asked?"

"About Cristine." He was indignant over her refusal to understand. "We're no closer to knowing the truth than we were."

"She barely knew about even Bridget," Bri reminded him. "Besides, when he left here, Peter may not have known about the baby."

"If you hadn't hurried me, maybe we could have found out." He stomped over to his vehicle, unlocked the door and fastened Cristine inside. "Where next?"

Bri climbed in and waited for him to join her.

"Just a minute, Ty," she began, when he shoved the key into the ignition. "We need to talk about this."

"What's to talk about? I want answers and I intend to get them." His belligerence dared her to argue with that.

"I want answers, too. But you can't force them out of people. They have to talk it out, go back in their memories. We're asking about two years ago. Can you remember what happened two years ago? Just like that!" She snapped her fingers.

His eyes flared, his mouth tightened. He was furious.

Bri laid a hand on his arm in a silent plea. "We're on the same side here. We both want answers. I just don't want to alienate anyone along the way."

"How am I alienating?" Fury laced his voice.

"You stomp in there with your list of questions and demand they answer you." Bri's frustration grew. "We have no legal status, no means to compel anyone. We just have to hope they'll remember something."

"She didn't." He motioned with his head toward the bank.

"She remembered quite a lot." Bri ticked the details off on her fingers. "Peter worked just long enough to support his habit of extreme sports. He went hiking with his girlfriend a lot."

"Big deal." He thumped the steering wheel with his palm. "Where does that get us? Exactly nowhere nearer to my goal."

"You are such a control freak!" Bri glared at him. "Stop focusing on *your* goal for a minute, slow down and think. If you spent almost every dime you made, how would you live?"

"Cheaply." He nodded. "Okay. So what?"

"Rappelling, heli-skiing, cross-country biking. All that stuff takes gear. Expensive gear. You wouldn't haul it around with you."

Ty's eyes opened wide. "So maybe he lived with some buddies?"

"Or maybe he stayed with his parents when he came to Calgary."

"We could ask the bank for his last known address." He grinned at the brilliance of it.

Bri smiled. "I already tried that. They won't give out personal information on employees." Briony dug out a biscuit for Cristine to munch on.

"So what now?"

Bri grinned, her thumb motioning back over her shoulder. "Lunch, I think."

He laughed. "Good idea. I know just the place."

Bri had to admit, the restaurant was perfect. Cristine pranced around the children's play area as if she owned it, inspecting each toy with a crow of pleasure.

Bri smiled as she sipped her coffee and watched the little girl work off some of her excessive energy.

"Makes you tired, doesn't it?" Ty cupped his mug in both hands. "I need to apologize. Again."

She could hardly believe it. "For what?"

"For trying to barrel ahead. For trying to force you and the rest of the world to conform to my way." He thrust out his hands, palm up. "I'm beginning to realize that you've given this whole search thing a lot of thought."

"Yes, I have. And each time I think I've found an answer, I run into another roadblock." She held his gaze. "It's just as frustrating to me as it is to you, Ty. But I think if we can plan ahead, try to anticipate the finer points of this situation, we can save ourselves some grief."

He frowned. "I don't know what you mean."

"I'll tell you." Bri sucked in a breath of courage. "But you're not going to like this," she said.

His eyes darkened. "Your point is?"

"I want to phone all twelve of the Grants listed in the phone book."

His eyes lit up. "Hey, great idea. We should be able to get through it in no time. I'll take the first six." He jerked his cell phone off his belt.

Bri reached out to stop him. "I meant that *I* want to do it."

His face froze into that same angry mask.

"Just listen for a moment, will you?"

He shrugged.

"What if we end up reaching his wife? Are we just going to blurt out that we think Peter had a child with someone else? Or what if he and his family are estranged? We've got to be careful about how we handle this, Ty."

"You're not very flattering, do you know that? It's kind of hard on my ego." He sipped his coffee thoughtfully. "All right. I'll admit you're somewhat better than I am at beating around the bush."

"That wasn't—"

"So go ahead and start phoning. I'll watch Cristine and take lessons from a pro. Or should I say 'prof'?"

Bri wasn't sure how to take his comments. Ty often kept his emotions bottled up inside. She took her list and her phone from her purse.

"I'll start with the only 'P. Grant' listed." She dialed. "Hello, is this the Grant residence? My name is Briony Green. I'm trying to reach a Mr. Peter Grant who formerly worked at…" She gave just enough information to make her enquiry sound official.

"Thank you so much for your time. I'm sorry I bothered you." She clicked off her phone, then placed a little *X* by the name. "No relation. Don't know him. This P. Grant—Philip, is eighty-four."

Ty nodded, his eyes steady. "Go ahead."

She phoned six more, all with the same response. No one had heard of Peter Grant.

For the third time in as many minutes, Cristine fell and burst into tears.

"She's tired," Ty murmured as he consoled her. "I think we'd better get out of here."

They gathered up their things, paid the bill and left the now-crowded restaurant.

"There's a park, just over there. Maybe she'd sleep if we spread out a blanket."

Ty frowned. "I didn't—"

"I did." Bri reached into the bag at her feet and drew out an old quilt. "I keep this in my car for just these emergencies. Something told me to bring it along today."

Ten minutes later, Cristine was cuddled up in her daddy's arms, fast asleep. Ty kept up his rhythmic stroking of her back, his face soft as he watched her.

"You know, it occurs to me that all of this is an exercise in futility." Bri smiled at his curious glance. "You are Cristine's father as certainly as I'm sitting here. She doesn't want or need any other. There's nothing anyone could give her that you haven't, Ty."

"Except a mother." The words whispered so low, barely penetrated the rustling trees surrounding them.

"I'm sure you could find her a mother if you set your mind to it," she teased.

He lifted his head. Bri caught her breath at the wealth of defeat, the glimmer of regret she saw in his eyes.

"I can't marry again. Not ever."

"You think that now," she murmured, hiding her own pain at the words. "But someday, when Andrea's loss isn't quite so sharp, you'll look around and realize you've met someone who has taken root in your heart."

"It won't matter how I feel. I'll never marry." His voice, hard-edged, chewed out the words. "I can't," he muttered, his chin resting on his chest.

Bri didn't know what to say, couldn't think of the words that would reach him. She'd assumed that he and Andrea were happy, that he was bereft at her death.

But now, listening to him here, she heard yearning.

Bri leaned over to press her fingers against his. "I don't understand, Ty."

He lifted his head, smiled wryly and nodded. "No, you probably don't." Like a mantle, his eyes shuttered out their emotion, closing his thoughts to her. "Go ahead and phone, Briony."

"Okay."

She wanted to reach out so badly, ached to understand what he was thinking. But she wouldn't pry. Ty was a private man. He handled his grief in his own way.

And she wasn't part of his world.

The knowledge pricked her, reminding her how foolish she was to let herself get drawn into their lives. Cristine was her niece, but Bri would be leaving soon. Ty was the child's father. He would do what was best for the little girl, regardless of the cost to himself.

But as Bri snuck a second look, watched him sitting on the hillside, alone, with only his daughter for comfort, she felt the bleakness of his soul reach out and touch her.

Ty Demens touched a chord in her heart that had never been heard before. He was true to himself and his daughter. He didn't hide the truth, or pretend.

But he was a single father, and no matter how much Bri loved Cristine, she could never again allow herself to be a mommy substitute. If she couldn't be loved for herself, she'd do without. One thing she'd learned from being dumped at the altar—she couldn't live with second best, not in her work and not in her personal life.

Slowly Bri dialed the number. And the next. And the next.

"There's no point," Ty hissed, as she kept making Xs on her list. "We're getting nowhere. We need to move on to the next step."

"This *is* the next step." Her frustration mounted. "You heard me on the phone, talking to the lawyers. They don't know anything. To their knowledge there was never any mention of a birth father."

"And none of these people know Peter." He sighed. "It's a dead end. We might as well toss in the towel."

Bri shook her head. "No, I'll see it through. I know you think I'm nitpicky and obsessed with details." She nodded. "I am. In my work you have to analyze every option."

He kept observing her, his face impassive.

"Believe me, Ty, I know my way isn't the only way. It's just the only way I know."

He lifted an eyebrow.

"When I'm in the lab, I don't toss out anything. I note every detail, run thousands of tests, until I'm absolutely certain my conclusion is correct. If I don't, I run the risk of missing a clue, a detail that could change the results."

"And you think checking out every one of those phone numbers will put us a step closer to figuring out whether or not I get to keep my daughter?" He shrugged. "Go ahead. Personally, I've given up hope."

Bri smiled, then leaned forward to brush the hair out of his eyes. "Don't ever do that, Ty. Remember, our God is a God of hope."

His hand reached up, grasped hers and clung. "Your faith shames me. Here I am, always demanding quick fixes. I want the answers to my questions now.'' His thumb brushed against her knuckles. "And here you are, quietly taking care of the details, waiting.''

He stared down at their entwined fingers, his face brooding. "How do you do that, Briony? How can you let go of the controls and let God take over?''

"Oh, Ty, you do ask the toughest questions.'' She smiled, breathy at the intensity of his gaze.

"Well?'' He waited, impatient to hear her answer.

Bri used both hands to cup his face, holding it so she could stare directly into his eyes.

"The truth?'' She stroked her thumb against his cheek. "The truth is, I never had the controls in the first place, Ty. There is only one God. I'm not Him.''

After a single surprised moment, he leaned forward and kissed her, his lips softly sweet as they touched hers.

When he drew away, Briony could barely breathe. She saw a glimmer of humor lurking behind his solemn stare.

"Always so logical,'' he murmured.

"Can't help it. That's who I am.'' Bri wished he'd kiss her again, yet she knew she couldn't let it happen. Her hands fell away.

"I know, and I'm glad.'' He bussed her nose. "Finish your list, Briony. Then we'll go see my mother.''

Briony tore her gaze from his and concentrated on the last three names. She got a nibble on number two.

"William? I see. No, sir, I didn't know that. Married? Oh, no, I didn't know that. I see. Yes, I'm sure it was.'' She felt Ty's interested glance but deliberately kept her focus on her list as the words flowed across the phone.

"I'm so sorry. And that happened when?" She scribbled down the information, listening as she did.

"I'm terribly sorry to have bothered you, but I thank you for your help. Yes, God bless you, too, Mr. Grant. Goodbye."

"Well? Aren't you going to finish the list?" Ty gathered Cristine's tiny body as if he meant to rise. He stopped when he caught sight of Bri's face. "What is it?"

"*William* Peter Grant died a year ago last August in Peru when he fell down a mountain."

Ty collapsed back onto the quilt. "Died?"

Bri watched as he assimilated the information, added up and came to his conclusion.

"He died before Cristine was born?" He waited for her nod. "But how do we know he's our Peter?" he murmured. "There has to be more than one Peter Grant in the world."

"He's the one we want. Apparently his fiancée used to call him Will." Bri held his gaze, her voice emphasizing the detail. "This fiancée worked in a hotel in Banff. They hoped to be married when Will/Peter returned after his *August* climbing stint."

"He didn't know about Cristine!" Ty stared at her, trying to work it all out. "He never knew he was going to be a father."

Bri nodded. "Apparently it took the authorities some time to verify who he was and notify the next-of-kin. That's why Bridget's diary talks of them being a family. She didn't find out until well into the winter. She must have been so worried."

They fell silent, thinking of the young man whose life had ended too soon.

"This means that there's no one to stop me from

being Cristine's father.'' Ty's eyes lit up with excitement as he gazed lovingly at his daughter, then gently laid her on the quilt. ''If I hold her, I'll wake her up. My hands are shaking.''

Seconds later, Bri watched the thrill of it drain away.

''His parents. Do they want Cristine, Bri? Do they even know about her?''

Relieved that he realized the influence Cristine's biological family might want to exert, Bri freely told him the rest of the story as she stood to ease the cramp in her legs.

''Peter's parents died when he was a little boy. His aunt and uncle raised him. The aunt died a couple of months ago. His uncle is moving into a senior's complex soon. I'm sure he'd be delighted to get to know Cristine, but I can't imagine that he'd try to seek custody.''

Ty struggled to his feet, hesitating to voice the words that had so long been denied. Bri reached out and hugged him, her heart brimming with thanksgiving.

''She's yours, Ty. All yours. She always has been. You just didn't know the secrets God had in store.''

His arm looped around her waist and held her clamped against his side. He bent his head and buried it in her hair, nuzzling the softness as he spoke.

''Thank you, Briony. Thank you for persisting and insisting and showing me the way. Thank you for giving my daughter back to me.''

They stood holding each other, peering down at the sleeping child.

''I didn't do it, Ty,'' Bri whispered after a long time. ''It was a God thing.''

She felt the rumble of laughter shake his chest before it burbled out.

"I'm just beginning to understand that, Bri. Thanks to you." He lifted his head, his eyes glowing. "Let's go tell my family, okay? We can have a party!"

Bri smiled and nodded, her eyes misty, as he picked up his daughter and kissed her awake.

She was happy for him. She was! Ty's world glowed new and full of joy. At last he was free of the worry that had plagued him for so long.

He had everything he needed to be happy.

But for Briony, the world was still the same. And she was still standing on the sidelines, watching.

Alone.

Chapter Nine

❧

"Ah! At last I meet the infamous Dr. Green." Ty's sister thrust out a hand. "I'm Giselle. My husband and son are away for the week, or I'd introduce you to them. I'm guessing you remember Mom."

Giselle led them into the living room, where Mrs. Demens sat perched on a recliner, her bandaged leg evident beneath the cuff of her brown shorts.

"Nan!" Cristine wriggled out of her father's arms and scrambled across the room to climb up beside her grandmother.

Bri smiled as the two rubbed noses, hugged and chattered nonstop.

"Please sit down, Dr. Green. You won't get a word in edgewise once those two have started." Giselle reached up to wrap her slim tanned arms around her brother's neck in a hug. "You look good," she told him, frankly appraising his blue jeans and shirt.

"Thank you. So do you." He leaned back and took a second glance. "Are you putting on weight?"

"Ty! What a thing to say." Bri immediately wished

she'd stemmed her sputter of disapproval. Mrs. Demens and Giselle both turned to glance curiously at her.

"Ignore him, Briony. Can I call you Briony?" Giselle didn't wait for a nod. "Ty always blurts out the first comment that comes into his doddering head."

"Doddering?" Ty glowered at her. "I'm not yet doddering, thank you very much."

"Well, you will be soon, Uncle Ty." Giselle grinned at him. "We're having another baby."

"About time, too." Ty's gruff voice couldn't hide his pleasure as he hugged her again. "Congratulations, sis."

"From me, too." Bri held out a hand. "It's wonderful news. Do you want a girl this time?"

Giselle patted her still-flat tummy. "I want whatever God gives me," she said simply. "I'll leave that decision up to someone with more knowledge than I possess."

Bri sipped her tea, smiling and nodding as the three of them teased one another, watching the family interactions, while she tried to hide the persistent ache in her heart.

"I understand you're starting a new job soon." Giselle sank down beside Bri, her elegant sundress flaring out around her bare brown legs. "That must be exciting."

"I've worked toward it for a long time." Bri couldn't say more without divulging how she dreaded leaving Ty and Cristine.

"Still, you jumped from the frying pan into the fire when you finished school and then took on Cristine." Giselle's eyes sought her niece, a glow of love lingering there. "I love Cristine dearly, but she's a handful."

"Yes, she is." Briony smothered a laugh when Cristine tested her father's "no" by trying to ride her grandmother's leg like a horse. "I've grown very fond of her."

"Is she a lot like your sister?" Giselle's big eyes held no guile. She was honestly curious.

"Quite a bit, actually. But I think she's more like Ty."

"Really?" Giselle frowned, lips puckered in a moue of displeasure. "That's too bad. How?"

A blush stung Bri's face as she realized Giselle knew she'd been studying Ty. She shrugged.

"I don't really know how to explain it. Her focus, I suppose. Once she sets her mind on something, she will not be dissuaded without a very good reason."

"Well, that's exactly like Ty and don't I know it!" Giselle winked at Bri, fully aware of her brother's interest in their conversation. "Hardheaded. Not to mention pushy, stubborn, intolerant and inflexible." She grinned at his frown. "Not that Cristine is like that. Yet."

"Cristine is sweet and innocent." He grinned at them. "And she's mine."

"You found out something!" Giselle squealed with excitement, folded her legs up under her and leaned forward. "Spill it."

He explained about their day.

"What an answer to prayer." Mrs. Demens heaved a relieved sigh. "Briony, my dear, you were sent straight from heaven."

"Bee." Cristine pulled herself onto the sofa and flopped into Bri's lap. "Bee," she hummed over and over, her fingers careful, delicate as they touched Briony's unfettered hair.

"She certainly loves you." Giselle exchanged glances with her mother. "If I leave my hair down, she pulls it."

Bri brushed her hand over the little girl's soft cheek. "She's learning that causes pain," she murmured, touching the bright curls so like her own. "Most of the time she's very careful."

"You've done wonders for her." Mrs. Demens's voice rang round the room. "I think it's time we did something for you. I doubt you've had a minute's peace with Ty's schedule." She tapped her forefinger against her chin. "Let me see."

Giselle got into the spirit of things.

"Why don't you take her dancing, Ty? You haven't been out in ages." She turned to Bri. "You like dancing, don't you? Ty's great at ballroom stuff. Don't ask me why. All he ever did was step on my toes when I tried to teach him."

"That's because you always had to lead." Ty laughed at Giselle's inelegant snort. "You're more of a control freak than I am."

"Worse?" Bri couldn't imagine it. She wasn't even aware she'd spoken until she caught Giselle's smug little smile. "I mean—"

"Never mind, honey. We all know Ty. And we love him in spite of his tendency to boss us all. Most of the time, anyway." Mrs. Demens ignored Ty's interruption. "Dinner and dancing, I think. Yes, that should give you both a break. Now, where, Giselle?"

"Montague's." Giselle didn't need a moment to think. "They've got a lovely dance floor. Friday is their best night."

"And you guys have the nerve to call me bossy?" Ty glared at them both. "We didn't bring clothes to go dancing. We were in town to do business. We simply stopped by to let Cristine have a visit.''

"Oh, Tyrel, do be quiet. I'm thinking.'' Mrs. Demens motioned her daughter over and the two of them began a lively discussion on whether Giselle's husband was Ty's size. "I'm sure it will do. There now, that's settled. I'll call for reservations. Giselle, you take Briony and find her a dress. You're about the same size.''

Two minutes later Bri found herself in the master bedroom, standing in front of a massive closet with no clear idea of how she'd arrived there.

"This, maybe? No, wait.'' Giselle rifled through the hangers and pulled out a long white gown with a tiny matching jacket. "This is perfect.''

"I can't wear this.'' Bri fingered the seed pearls stitched to the jacket, her eyes huge. "What if I spilled something on it?''

Giselle shrugged. "Then we'll get it cleaned. Here's the matching bag. Now, what about shoes? I think my feet are bigger than yours.''

"Not by much.'' Bri touched the filmy chiffon, longing to try it on yet knowing she shouldn't. She was a scientist. This gown belonged on a model, or a movie star.

"How about these?'' Giselle held out a pair of strappy white sandals.

"They're lovely,'' Bri said honestly. And far too high. Bri's shoes never had heels that high.

"They're ridiculous, really. I never did wear them much.'' Giselle kicked off her sandal and thrust out one foot. "I have ugly toes.''

Bri didn't see anything wrong with Giselle's toes. But there wasn't really a nice way to say that. Anyway, she didn't have time. Giselle immediately launched into speech.

"You and my brother seem to get along. He doesn't usually respond well to my teasing." She settled onto the middle of her vast bed, full of questions. "Is it hard for you to deal with him?"

Bri blinked, sat down on a nearby chair and studied Ty's sister. "Hard?" she repeated.

"Does he get mad at you when everything doesn't happen exactly as he wants it?"

"No. Not usually." She smiled. "Though, to tell you the truth, I'm not sure I'd have noticed if he did. I'm pretty focused myself."

Giselle laughed merrily. "Good," she cheered. Her smile faded. "He had to be pretty controlled with Andrea, be the strong, sensible one. You know?" She tipped her head to one side like an inquisitive sparrow. "It's good to see him respond to another woman."

Bri had to stop this. "Oh, but I'm not—" Hmm. How *did* one tell Ty's sister that she wasn't interested in being a stand-in for her niece's mommy?

"Not what? Another woman?" Giselle blinked. "Of course you are. And it's very clear that my brother is fond of you."

Fond of her? Bri shook her head.

"I simply help out with Cristine. Nothing more."

"Do you really believe that?" Giselle's kind glance stopped any response Bri would have made. "I can see that you care for him, Briony. It's in your eyes whenever you look at him."

"Giselle, I like your brother. I think he's doing a wonderful job with Cristine, managing a difficult situation more adeptly than a lot of men could." She took a deep breath. "But come the end of the month,

I'm leaving to start a new life. It's one I've dreamed of for years. I'll see Cristine and Ty, of course, as often as I can."

"But that's it?"

"That's all it can be. I love my niece. I care very much about her future. But I can't pretend to be her mother. I've got to move on with my life, just as Ty will move on with his."

"To move anything, Ty will have to be prodded." Giselle chewed on the edge of a nail. "He doesn't talk about Andrea a lot, but I know it wasn't an ideal marriage."

Bri knew she shouldn't listen, but how could she escape? Giselle seemed set on pouring out her heart.

"I'm not sure there are any ideal marriages."

"Maybe not. But it works far better when you're pulling together rather than apart." She broke off her discussion to smile at her mother, who was peeking around the doorway. "Hi."

"Find anything spiffy?" Her mother picked up the hanger with the glistening white outfit and nodded. "Yes, this is perfect."

She laid the dress back down, then turned to Bri. "Thank you so much for standing in for me. I'm quite sure I've never told you how much I appreciate all you've done. These past weeks have been so nice. I've done nothing but laze around."

Ty's mother wrapped Briony in a hug that made her feel warm and cared for.

"I'm glad I could help. I'd do more if I could…"

"I know you promised to be at work the second of July. We wouldn't dream of asking you to put your life on hold any longer." Mrs. Demens sat down on the bed, easing her heavy cast up onto the pretty peach quilt. "Cristine's taken everything in her stride, and I'm sure that's due to you. She's going to miss you."

"I'll miss her, too." Bri didn't dare think about that now. She was grateful when Giselle motioned her out of the room, one eye on her mother's lined face.

"You relax for a minute, Mom," she said before she closed the door. "Briony and I will help Ty with Cristine."

Since Ty didn't object to his sister and mother organizing their evening, Briony didn't feel comfortable about protesting. When the time came, she slipped into Giselle's gorgeous dress and shoes, then obediently sat and let Ty's sister fiddle with her hair.

"There. You look lovely, Briony. Ty's going to be so proud to escort you."

Bri stared at herself in the mirror and swallowed. She felt pretty, as if she were a beautiful woman going out with a wonderful man. She wasn't beautiful, of course. But Ty was handsome. How long had it been since he'd dated?

She realized she'd attended only group functions since her almost-wedding six years ago. Of course, her studies meant she devoted hours to her career, but still—was this truly the path she would tread for the rest of her life? Always alone, always on guard.

The thought scared her.

"Is there someone special in your life?" Giselle put away the brush and spray, her conversation casual.

Special? Bri shook her head.

"No. I was just thinking to myself that it's been a long time since I've been out with anyone."

"Oh." Giselle plopped down on the bench beside her. "Why?"

How much should she tell? Bri decided the bare bones were enough.

"I was engaged once."

"Really? What happened?"

"My fiancé decided his ex-wife would make a better mother for his son than I would." The bitterness behind those words surprised her. Surely she'd forgiven Lance?

"I'm so sorry." Giselle's hand covered hers in a gentle squeeze. "But you can't let that stop you from opening your heart to someone else."

"I haven't." Bri smiled at her raised eyebrow. "Well, not really." She explained about the child. "Of course, I eventually realized that God expected me to use the talents he's given me. That means concentrating on my work, excelling at what I do best."

"But—"

"I'm not really very good at motherhood, Giselle. People always say it's instinctive, but it's not for me. I have to have it all charted out or I mess up." She rolled her eyes. "Do you know that I gave Cristine a whole apple once?"

Giselle burst out laughing. "Knowing Cristine, she probably sunk in her teeth, too."

"She did."

"I can just picture it." Her smile faded, her eyes serious. "But don't you see, Briony? You've been a wonderful mother for Cristine. I'm sure it hasn't been easy, but you've figured out what you need to know. Cristine certainly hasn't suffered. God has blessed you. He can use whatever you do if you hand it over to him."

"I suppose."

"It's not only that, is it? There's something else about caring for Cristine that bothers you."

Bri simply stared at Giselle and let her figure it out for herself.

A moment later, Giselle's eyes widened. "It's not the same as before, Bri. Ty won't yank Cristine out of your life, forbid you to ever see her again. He knows how much you love her."

"I know. After today, he'll never worry about losing Cristine to someone else. She has her fat little fingers wrapped tightly around his heart." Bri kept her head bent, her eyes on her plain unvarnished nails.

"Then, what's bothering you so much?" Giselle waited patiently, while Bri sorted through her thoughts. "I'd like to help if I can."

"I know. And I appreciate it." She stopped, then after a moment said, "It's hard to explain."

What was she afraid of? Bri wasn't sure she knew anymore. She was only aware of a deep persistent ache and a feeling that moving to Calgary wouldn't cure it.

"I guess I'm afraid to let myself want anything too much," she admitted at last.

"I'm sure that's perfectly natural. You've lost a sister, your parents, all your connections." She studied Briony. "What else?"

"You're an awful lot like your brother, you know." Bri sighed. "I'm not sure I can explain this without sounding smugly superior."

"I don't think you're smugly superior."

Bri smiled. "You will," she promised with a sigh. "You see, I was always the brain. I found my studies incredibly easy. Bridget didn't. It—caused a lot of strife. I always felt 'not normal.' Bridget had tons of boyfriends, lots of dates. She was the life of the party.

I never figured that stuff out. Didn't want to, if the truth were known. I was totally focused on my books.''

"So you hid behind your brains?"

Bri nodded, cheeks burning. ''As I look back now, I realize that I avoided trying to be part of her circle because that was where Bridget excelled.''

"And you didn't want to steal it from her." Giselle nodded. "I think that's commendable."

"Not really. I never let anyone see that I wanted more from life than to be the class valedictorian, the university's top student, the professor's pet project.'' Her voice dropped to a whisper. ''I never let them see me.''

"Not anybody?"

"Well, two others knew." Bri smiled, remembering. "There were three of us who roomed together in college. Each of us got dumped at the altar and so we banded together.'' She glanced up at Giselle. ''Clarissa and Blair are happily married now. They've made peace and moved on. I'm the only one who's still out in the cold.''

"But you don't have to be! I'm sure there are any number of men willing to take you out." Giselle straightened a drooping curl. "You don't have to be alone, Briony.''

"Don't I?" She couldn't afford to cling to the hope Giselle offered. "That's the crux of the issue, you see. All these years I've focused on my work and been perfectly happy. It wasn't until I met Ty and began to care for Cristine that I even questioned my future. I'd just accepted that God meant for me to handle life alone. It's what I'd always done.''

"Uh-huh." Giselle's lips curled up in a knowing smile. "And now that's not enough?"

"It has to be!" Bri concentrated her thoughts, organizing them so she could clearly express something she wasn't sure of herself. "I'd make a lousy mother. I get too focused on work because that's my purpose. That's where my strengths lie. That's where God wants me to be—in the lab."

Giselle stood, her hand gentle on Briony's shoulder. "Are you certain of that?"

"Yes."

"Then, I have only one thing to say. Sometimes we believe God is sticking with the tried and true, when in reality He wants to branch out and treat us to something special. But He can't, because we're stuck in our fear."

"I'm not sure I understand that. I believe God has a purpose for everything. I know there's nothing He'll give me that I can't handle."

Giselle snorted. "Of course He'll give you things you can't handle!" she insisted. "If He didn't, why would we ever have to call on Him for help?"

"Well, that's sort of what I meant. I was trying to say I believe God has everything under control."

"Hmm. Yes." Giselle nodded slowly. "But you're trying to understand his control from your earthly viewpoint. Just as Ty has always done. My brother is so certain that Cristine is the only child he'll ever have that he clings to her out of fear. He can't see beyond that." She shook her head.

"God isn't that small, Bri. He's bigger than anything we can imagine, and sometimes, every once in a while, he wants to surprise us with his magnificent abundance. We simply have to let him."

"Are you guys ever going to be finished in there?" Ty's low voice rumbled through the closed door. "Our reservation is in fifteen minutes."

Giselle tugged open the door, motioned to Bri and said, "Ta-da!"

Ty scrutinized every move, as Bri stood and glided toward him. His dark eyes glowed with admiration. "Wow!"

"Doesn't she look great?" Giselle rose on her tiptoes to kiss his cheek. "You look nice, too. For a brother. It's a good thing my husband is your size." She brushed a speck of lint off his shoulder. "Though I do believe he's just a tad more handsome than you."

Ty ignored her. "Ready?" he murmured, one hand outstretched to Bri.

"Yes." She let his fingers wrap around hers, warming them. Then she caught Giselle's knowing look.

"Remember what I said, Briony."

Bri nodded. "I will, and thank you. For everything."

Cristine didn't even notice their departure, she was so busy with the crayons her grandmother was laying out on the table.

Ty helped Bri into an unfamiliar car, which he said was his sister's. Once on the way, he tuned the radio to some soft music, then glanced sideways at her.

"I'm almost afraid to ask," he muttered. "But what, exactly, did my sister say?"

She laughed. "Worried?"

"Yes. I've learned over the years to be worried whenever Giselle locks herself in the bedroom with a woman I'm about to take to dinner."

"Ah." She hid her smile. "Have there been so many?"

He frowned at her, but answered. "Some. Not that many." He shrugged. "Andrea and I grew up together. I didn't date a lot."

"You knew she was the woman for you from the beginning?" Ty's hesitation made her study him more closely. "Did I say something wrong?"

He shook his head. "No, but tonight I'd rather forget the past and concentrate on enjoying ourselves. We probably won't get another break like this for a long time."

I won't, anyway. I'll be gone in less than two weeks, and you'll have Cristine all to yourself.

The thought stung Bri into silence.

"Do you like to dance?"

Bri blinked. "Um, I guess. I don't think I'm very good at it." Something twigged. "You ballroom dance, they said."

"I use to. Haven't done it for a while."

Bri choked. "I'll embarrass you terribly."

"We're not in competition, Bri. We're just going to enjoy ourselves."

She sat, mulling that over. "How did *you* ever get interested in ballroom dancing?"

He grinned at her, his eyes twinkling. "Doesn't seem like a macho thing, does it?"

He laughed out loud as the color rose to her cheeks. For once he looked free of the memories, happy to be in her company.

"Believe me, I didn't think so, either, until my football coach pointed out how fast those guys moved, how intricate their footwork was. Coordination was a problem for me back then."

She stared. "I don't believe it."

He nodded. "Oh, yeah. I grew so fast, I couldn't make my feet and my body move in sync."

Bri got lost in the picture of Ty's lean, lithe body ever stumbling.

"You didn't answer my question." He held her gaze. "What did Giselle say?"

"We were talking about me, mostly. I'm afraid I'm not very good at the social stuff," she explained.

He frowned. "You do that a lot, you know."

"Do what?"

"Put yourself down. As if being smart is somehow bad or less than optimal. There's nothing wrong with using the mind God gave you, Bri."

"Especially if that's all He gave me." She muttered the words to herself, wishing she'd never agreed to go out. How was she going to make light conversation when she felt so out of place?

"It isn't all He gave you." Ty's soft, assured voice penetrated the radio's violin concerto. "He gave you true beauty, inside and out. He gave you insight and understanding for others. He gave you love for your sister, enough to ensure you would check up on her daughter. You've been royally blessed, Briony."

She stared. She couldn't help it. His words brimmed with sincerity. He wasn't trying to flatter her; he really believed what he was saying.

"I—I never thought of it like that before." She swallowed. "I guess I have been blessed."

"Yes." He nodded, certainty swirling in his eyes as he sat waiting for the traffic light to turn green. "And so have I. Cristine is the best thing that's ever happened to me. I'll be eternally grateful for her in my life."

"And you don't want anything else?"

His eyes dulled, the shine disappeared. He turned back to concentrate on the traffic. "We don't always get what we want, Briony. Sometimes we have to be happy with what we have."

"That's funny."

"Funny?" He looked grim. "Why?"

"Giselle just finished telling me that I settle for too little. She basically told me that I was afraid to accept what God wanted to give me because I won't look beyond my preconceptions." Bri frowned. "At least, I think that's what she was saying."

Ty made a face. "Giselle is thrilled with her life right now. She wants everyone to be as happy as she is. She doesn't understand that God doesn't always give you what you ask for."

"I think she was implying that He wants to give more than we could even ask or think." Bri contemplated that, while Ty found a parking spot, opened her door and helped her out of the car.

"Let's forget about my sister for a while," he muttered as he guided her to the restaurant's front door. "She always thinks she knows best—and that bugs me."

"By all means, let's not have you bugged." Bri grinned at him, hoping to tease him out of his grumpiness. "If you think God wants you to be happy with your life the way it is, who am I to question it?"

He gave her a hard look, then turned to speak to the maître d'. Once they were seated, however, his manner changed completely.

"You're very beautiful, Briony. I don't have the right words to tell you how lovely you look tonight."

"Thank you." She fiddled with the little evening

bag, screwing up enough courage to meet his stare. "I suppose you want to dance?"

He shrugged. "If you do. The music is good and the floor's not too crowded." A dreamy romantic ballad underscored his words.

Bri sighed. "Just don't expect me to follow any fancy moves," she said as she set down her bag. "Plain and basic, that's me."

He held out her chair, then slipped a hand around her waist as he guided her to the floor. As she moved into his arms and began to sway to the music, her footsteps following his lead, Bri relaxed. It felt so right, so good, to be here like this.

"I don't think I've ever known anyone less plain or less basic," he murmured into her ear, his lips grazing the skin laid bare by her upswept hair. "You're an amazing woman, Briony Green."

She tilted her head up. Her eyes widened as they met the intent look in his. "Tonight, with Giselle's finery, you mean."

He shook his head, his eyes never leaving hers. "Tonight, last week when you got caught in the rain, the first day with carrot goop splattered all over your clothes. Yours is the kind of beauty that withstands all the tests."

She didn't know what to say, so she said nothing.

When the third song started, Ty enfolded her in his arms and danced her out onto the patio. The rich blackness of the night provided the perfect backdrop for the tiny white lights scattered across the hedge surrounding them and flung high up into the sheltering cedar trees. A hundred miniature lanterns swung gently in the breeze.

"Cristine and I were blessed the day you came into

our lives. I'm sorry you have to go, but you'll always be welcome to come and visit.''

Visit? Bri closed her eyes as the truth slammed into her heart.

She was totally, completely and stupidly in love with Tyrel Demens—a man who could not forget his dead wife.

How could God have let this happen?

Chapter Ten

Briony's sudden silence mystified Ty. He finished the dance, ordered their meals and kept up a light patter of conversation, hoping she'd come back from whatever place her mind had journeyed to.

Tonight he realized just how exquisite she was. Every time he held her, every time her cheek grazed his chest, every time her breath brushed across his neck, another stab of pain darted into his heart.

Why had God brought Briony into his life now, when it was too late?

"Is anything wrong?" He studied the delicate way she held her fork, blinked as it gleamed in the candlelight, observed her face softened by the shadows.

"Wrong?" She swallowed, staring at him in confusion.

"You seem distracted, worried. Is the salmon not to your taste?"

"It's fine. Thank you."

He watched, saw how desperately she searched for a topic to keep him busy, something deep enough that he wouldn't question her about her irregular breathing, or the odd stares she tried to hide.

"I was just thinking about this afternoon."

"Cristine's father, you mean." He frowned. He set down his fork; his appetite had suddenly fled.

"You are Cristine's father, Ty. Her only father." She reached out to touch him, then quickly pulled her hand back, as if afraid. "Yes, I was thinking about Peter. I remembered something Bridget wrote—'Will isn't enough.'" She shook her head.

"I didn't understand it then. I thought she was referring to something else. But now I believe she was talking about her relationship with Peter. Remember his uncle said he was really William?"

"Yes, I see. So there may be several other references to him that you didn't pick up on." He sipped his coffee thoughtfully, hating to rehash that time again, but knowing there could yet be answers they hadn't uncovered. "You think it was only after she found out he was dead that she decided to let Cristine be adopted?"

Briony nodded. "I'm fairly certain of it, now that I consider what I've read. She writes at length of her desire for a 'real' father for her baby. That must be why she connected with Andrea. She believed the two of you offered the most opportunity for her daughter."

It made a weird sort of sense to Ty now. Andrea must have known Bridget was having second thoughts about keeping her baby. Reality hit him squarely between the eyes.

"But that means she must have told Andrea that Peter was dead!" Ty glared at the tablecloth, his face grim as he fit the pieces together. "Why wouldn't Andrea have told me? Why make me go through this hell of wondering?''

"I don't know, Ty."

Her soft voice shamed him.

"I'm sorry, Briony. None of this is your problem, yet I keep dragging you into my messed-up life." He tossed down his napkin. "Would you like to go for a walk before dessert? They have lovely grounds here."

She placed her own napkin on the table and stood immediately.

Ty led her out onto the patio and beyond, down the tiny path that followed a brook. He said nothing as his mind raged over the injustice of it.

Why hadn't Andrea shared the truth? Why deceive him? There was no benefit, no possible good to come of keeping the truth from him. Except to keep him hanging, worrying, wondering.

"Are you all right?"

They'd stopped beside a little stone bridge. Briony stood in front of him, one hand on his arm, her face sad in the wash of moonlight.

"I'm so sorry, Ty. If I could, I'd erase it all, take the pain myself."

Her words unleashed a torrent of longing that Ty stemmed by crushing her against him, hanging on to her as if she were a lifeline in his confused, upset world.

"Thank you," he whispered, breathing in the sweet flowery scent that clung to her. Long ago, when he'd first thought about marriage, Ty had imagined life with someone like Briony.

She was everything he'd ever dreamed about in a woman. Able to stand up for herself, but still capable of helping someone else. She didn't play games, didn't pretend, didn't prevaricate. Briony lived truth. She dealt in facts, not half truths.

"Ty?" She lifted her head, her sapphire eyes glittering with unshed tears. "I'm sorry I brought all this trouble on you. I wish I'd never gone to Banff!"

"Don't say that." He lifted a finger to brush it across her wet lashes. "You've done so much for us. You've given me the security I needed with Cristine."

"But I've caused you so much pain." Her voice whispered across his skin as her lips touched the hand lingering near her mouth.

"Not you, Briony. Never you." Ty bent and swept his mouth across hers, offering a kiss of reassurance. But that wasn't what he wanted at all, he realized the moment his mouth locked on hers.

He wanted to erase the shadows in her eyes, to kiss away the tears and pain he saw on her face. He wanted to ease her loss over her parents' and Bridget's deaths.

All of this and more Ty sought to convey with his embrace. But more than that, he tried to show her how much he cared for her. He tried to express the joy she brought to his life with her delight over accomplishing the simplest things. He caressed her for her patience and understanding with Cristine.

But by the time he finally pulled away, Ty knew that he'd kissed Briony Green because of something far deeper than simple appreciation. As he cradled her small, compact body in his arms, felt her fingers tangle in his hair, heard her sigh of pleasure as she nestled against him, Ty knew that he'd kissed Briony Green because he loved her. And that was a mistake.

So now what did he do?

Ty stood transfixed, holding the woman of his dreams in his arms as the evening surrounded them like a dark velvet cloak. He pretended to consider his options. In reality, he had only one.

The truth.

He refused to play games, to lead Bri on, to pretend that there could ever be anything between them.

"Briony?" He eased her away, his heart wrenching the rapturous glow on her face. "I need to talk to you."

"Talk?" She leaned back, her arms clasped behind his neck. "You kiss me like that and then you want to talk?"

"We have to." He removed his hands, then gently led her toward a bench that sat sheltered under the drooping shelter of a weeping birch tree. "Here. Sit down."

"All right."

Slowly, her natural reserve reasserted itself. Perversely, Ty was glad. She'd need that calm reserve in a minute. He sat down on the other end of the bench and placed his hand over hers where they lay clasped in her lap.

"I shouldn't have kissed you, Briony."

"Why not?" She frowned, her eyes darkening. "Is it because of your wife?"

"In a way." He searched for a way to tell her. "But it's more that I have no right to kiss you."

"I understand. You loved her too much. Kissing me is like a betrayal." She drew her hands away, hid them under the folds of her skirt. "I'm sorry."

His heart contracted at the pain in her eyes.

"I did love Andrea," he admitted. "Perhaps not the way you mean, exactly, but in my own way I cared deeply for her."

"You don't have to go on. I've said I understand."

She would have stood then, but he stopped her with one hand on her arm.

"You don't understand, Briony. But I'd like you to." He waited until she subsided, fully aware that she now sat as far from him as possible. Time to tell the truth.

"Andrea had problems. To compensate, she made herself a dreamworld and she made me a part of it. She wanted children. She would be their mother, love them, care for them, do all the things her own mother never did. She was going to be different. She pulled herself out of her depression with a huge effort, and we got married."

He sensed that it hurt her to hear this. And why not? It hurt him to rehash this sad story. He plodded on.

"In the beginning we were very happy. I loved my work and Andrea was busy fixing the house. It didn't dawn on me, at first, that anything was wrong. I was a fool!"

She laid a hand on his arm. "Don't blame yourself, Ty."

"It was my fault."

She simply shook her head. "Go on."

"Every month she'd be so full of hope. And every month those hopes would be dashed when she learned she wasn't pregnant." Ty's face burned with shame. Was it right to tell her all this? But how else would Briony understand his determination never to marry again?

"It was like living on a roller coaster," he whispered, as all the old ache and regret he'd thought long buried swept back over him. "High hope, then crashing disappointment. She was devastated each time it happened."

"As were you."

He nodded slowly. "Yes, I guess I was. I'd always wanted kids. I agreed to see a specialist, agreed to have tests, agreed to try whatever they suggested." He stopped, searched for an appropriate way to explain.

"When our last hope was gone, we crashed for a while and tried to move on with our lives. Then Andrea decided we should adopt."

"You didn't want to?"

He looked at her, saw the commiseration and empathy in her eyes. The words poured out of their own volition.

"I just wanted to get off the roller coaster. I compensated with work, lots of it. I know that didn't help her, but I couldn't stand to see her immobilized by the horrible world of pain she suffered. I couldn't stand to watch the love in her eyes die, to see the blame she tried to mask."

"Why should she blame you? You both wanted children."

"It was my fault. I'm the one who made it impossible for my wife to be the mother she'd always dreamed of. Do you understand, Briony? I killed her dreams because I can never be a father."

"Oh, Ty." Her arms came around him then as she scooted across the bench to hold him. "I'm so sorry."

Ty let himself revel in her compassion for just one precious moment. Then he carefully drew away.

"We filled out all the papers for adoption, only to learn that it could take up to five years. Andrea begged me to take her overseas, to adopt a child from one of those countries you hear so much about." Ty raked a hand through his hair.

"I wouldn't do it. I couldn't! She had so many problems already. How would she deal with a foreign child who couldn't immediately do and say all the things she'd dreamed about? She was so fragile, emotionally drained, living on the edge.'' He shook his head. ''Even if we could have afforded it, I couldn't take the chance.''

''What did you do?''

He knew she knew. He could hear it in her voice.

''I buried myself in work. I got her the best help I could, made sure she went to every appointment, watched her take her medication. And I prayed. Desperately. I begged God to help.'' The shame of it still ate at him.

''I wanted out, Briony. I wanted to forget it all. Failing that, I just wanted her to be happy, to make the best of what we had. If an adoption worked out, okay. If not, we had each other.'' He almost laughed at the stupidity of those dreams.

''Andrea was furious, said I'd never cared about what she needed. We argued constantly. Then I had to leave for the fire.''

''And she found Bridget.''

''I guess.'' Ty clasped his head in his hands. ''We'd spent every dime we had trying to get a baby, and we were left scrounging. Nothing was the way I wanted. I took every overtime shift I could to get the bills paid off. I was bitter that we'd spent so much and gotten nothing.'' He swallowed. ''I hated God for doing that to us.''

''Ty!''

''I did. In a way, I still do.'' He implored her to understand. ''He's the God of everything, Briony. He could have eased her through it all without the loathing and pain. He could have given her a child—sent us a baby.''

"He did.'' Briony's tears fell unashamed onto her cheeks. "He sent you Cristine.''

Ty shook his head, fury burning in the depths of his heart. The anger and bitterness had never died. It welled up now with a fierceness that grabbed him and hung on.

"God didn't send Cristine,'' he told her. "Andrea went out and found Cristine. Do you think they would have met if Andrea hadn't been so actively seeking a child?''

He could hardly bear to think it even now. All that time she'd kept it a secret from him, kept Cristine's true identity and parenthood a secret that he should have shared. Why? Revenge?

Ty couldn't deal with that now. He shoved it away.

"God did nothing, Briony. Nothing!'' The words spilled out in an angry tirade. "He let us hang there for years, vainly hoping. And I've spent another year-and-a-half wondering if Cristine would be ripped out of my arms. Is that love?''

He glared at her, willing her to understand. His fingers closed about her arm in a tight grip.

But Briony didn't flinch, didn't look away. Her blue eyes stared calmly into his, her face wet with tears.

"Yes, Ty. That is love. God's love. I don't understand why it had to be like that, I don't understand why He didn't alter the circumstances, but He had a reason.''

Ty knew his face reflected his disgust at her answer. He didn't even try to mask it. Just this once he wanted it out, all of it. He wanted someone else to understand how betrayed he felt by the God he'd trusted day after day for most of his adult life.

But not anymore. He would never hope again.

"Some love! And was it also this divine love that took Andrea after she'd had only six weeks with the child she'd always wanted? Was that an expression of this *godly love?*"

She nodded, eyes never leaving his. "Yes, Ty."

His lips twisted at her quiet response. "Well, I don't want that kind of love, do you hear me? I don't need some kind of judge standing over me, ready to snatch away anything I set my heart on." His fists clenched uselessly as anger surged through him.

Bri's soft voice shattered the hate. "Do you think you can stop God from doing His will by refusing to accept it?" She smiled gently. "It won't work, my dear."

He wondered at the endearment, but didn't stop to question it. "Then I don't want any part of Him."

"What do you want, Ty?"

The words threw him. He knew she wasn't blaming, wasn't trying to convince him. Maybe she didn't understand.

"Look, I know I didn't handle things well. I know I messed up and disappointed Andrea when I should have been there for her. If I could change it, I would. But I can't."

"So you're going to press on to the future and hope you manage better next time?"

She didn't understand. He'd have to lay it out plainly. "There won't be a next time, Bri. I'll never marry again. I won't watch another woman go through what Andrea did, hoping maybe God will relent, believing things will be different." Ty shook his head.

"I won't take that chance again." He clenched his jaw, stemming the rest of his bitter tirade. Briony didn't deserve it. "I'll raise Cristine and be happy with that."

She studied him, amazement pleating her smooth forehead. "Do you realize what you're saying, Ty? You're telling God that if He won't play by your rules, you won't play with Him!"

He sat silent, refusing to debate the issue.

"You can't do it, Ty. God is in control, not you. He's not going to apologize for running His world the way He wants it run. He's the boss, He's *God!* You're not. Just because you decide He was wrong doesn't change the facts. He wants you, He loves you. He has the best in store for you. What you do with that is up to you."

Ty got up and paced, his mind racing over what she'd said. "When you put it that way, it sounds childish," he muttered in disgust.

"It is childish!" Bri grinned at his sour look. "But we're His children. I guess we're entitled to act like it once in a while."

He couldn't let her brush it off so easily. "I don't accept that, Briony. He didn't have to let it happen. He could have stopped it, all of it."

She rose slowly, the white gossamer fabric floating around her as she stood in front of him. Her blue eyes glowed with an inner fire.

"If God had changed it, I'd never have met you," she whispered as her fingers drifted over his cheek. "I'd never have known how wonderful Cristine was, I'd never have understood my sister, I'd never have fallen in love with you."

"No!" Ty reared back, aghast at her words.

"Yes, it's true. I only realized it myself tonight. I had no intention of telling you because I was afraid."

He frowned. Afraid? "Of me?"

"Of your using me. Of being nothing more than a convenient caregiver for Cristine. Of letting myself love and then get hurt."

She brushed her fingers through his hair, her touch gently addicting. Ty froze at that soft caress. Bri's gentle fingers said more than any words she might whisper on the night air.

"I believed God didn't want me to know anything about love, Ty. After my fiancé dumped me and I couldn't see his son anymore, I figured God intended for me to devote myself to my career. And I have." She smiled. "Sometimes too much."

"There's nothing wrong with that." He shifted so her hands fell to his shoulders. Just for a minute, Ty let himself relax.

"Actually, I've realized there is. God doesn't do things poorly. He doesn't withhold His blessings to those who love Him."

Her fingers soothed his throbbing head.

"God's ways are perfect and He wants well-rounded people in His kingdom. Locking myself away because I was afraid to get hurt wasn't healthy. Pretending my career met all my needs wasn't, either."

Ty wanted to protest, but something silenced him.

"Can I tell you something? A secret I've never shared with anyone?" She didn't wait for his nod. "I know it doesn't jibe with my image at all. People think I'm strong and self-sufficient, that I don't notice others."

Her tremulous smile lifted the corners of her generous mouth. "I notice, Ty. I always have. When my friend Blair had to leave school to raise her little boy, I was envious. Her fiancé had taken off, but she had someone who loved her just because she was his mother.'' A faint smile touched her pale pink lips.

''This was your college roommate?''

She nodded, eyes misty.

''My other roomie, Clarissa, married a man with four kids. I thought she was the luckiest woman in the world to have her house full of people who always needed her for something.''

Ty closed his eyes, sucked in a breath for control. Here it was again. The same female need to have a baby. Briony was no different from Andrea, though he ached to pretend otherwise.

If he'd had any doubts about the need to push Briony Green away, they were gone. Things would be the same with Bri. If he took the love she offered, if he dared to care for her, she would end up agonizing just as Andrea had, wasting her life craving for something he couldn't give her.

''You're not listening to me, Ty.''

He opened his eyes, stared at his feet, nodded. ''Sure I am. You were saying how much having a baby meant to you. Which is exactly why I started out by saying I have no right to kiss you.''

''Shut up, Tyrel.''

He blinked, caught a glimpse of her face and swallowed.

''It isn't about babies,'' she hissed, blue eyes spitting sparks. ''It isn't about parenthood. It's about being loved. Unconditionally. It's something Cristine offers every time she hugs you or sees me or greets her grandmother. That's what I longed for, that's what my sister found and that's what I want from my life.''

Ty needed to get away. He ached to turn tail and run like a coward, but Bri's intense gaze wouldn't permit any backing down. All he could do was stand there.

"I think I've finally figured it out," she whispered, her eyes wide with understanding. "I love you. Next to that, my career comes a distant second."

He opened his mouth, but she forestalled him. "I know you can't or won't love me back. I know you think you're mad at God and you want to tell Him how to manage His world. I know you're scared and hurt and, most of all, angry." She wrapped her arms around his waist and hugged him so tightly he felt it straight through to his heart.

"But that doesn't change a single thing, Tyrel Demens. I still love you."

She leaned back, arms still hugging his waist, eyes sparkling with a joy that would not be suppressed.

"You can't control it. You can't quash it or make it go away, or pretend it isn't there. There's not a single thing you can do to stop me from feeling this way. I love you, Ty Demens. So there!"

Ty unwrapped her arms, set her gently away. He stood and walked to the edge of the water, stared into its tumbling froth.

"It won't work, Briony," he whispered, shaken at the havoc in his mind, his soul. "I can't have anything to do with you."

"Okay."

He turned to stare at her, stunned by her acceptance.

"All these years, Ty, I've never even met anyone I specially liked, let alone fell in love with."

"And?"

She spread her hands wide. "This love, it's a God

thing, Ty. He brought me to Banff, He organized Cristine's adoption, He's been in it all along.''

"So now what?" Ty wished he could steal some of that hope that glowed in her eyes and claim it as his own. But he couldn't. He was powerless.

"So now I'm going to wait and see what God wants to do with it,'' she told him with a cheeky grin.

"You'd dump your career, just like that?" He couldn't believe it. "Give it all up, just to be a wife and mother? All those years of work?''

Bri shook her head, tapped one finger against his brow. "Ty, think about it. He's God. I keep telling you, He knows what He's doing.'' She laughed at his scowl. "God didn't send me to school for all those years so He could ignore me. He's got a plan, He'll work it out. I just have to trust.''

Ty stared at her for a long time, trying to wrap his brain around what she said. But he couldn't. The fear, the hurt, the pain—they all crowded out whatever little faith he'd once enjoyed.

Briony made him consider things he had no right to imagine. He didn't want to go back to being that empty man he'd once been—beaten, broken, helpless. He wanted to keep his life on the track he'd set, care for Cristine, get the promotion at work. He wanted to know what tomorrow held.

Pretending he would get what he wanted without striving for it was a pipe dream.

"Come on, it's time to go. We still have to drive home.''

Bri followed him from the restaurant without a word. They drove through the city to Giselle's, changed and said their farewells. Then, with a sleeping

Cristine firmly belted into her car seat, Ty drove back toward Banff.

Unless directly questioned, Briony remained silent, eyes watchful on the road ahead. Ty turned the radio on, glad for the distraction. But as he caught a glimpse of Briony's serene profile in the flash of lights from an oncoming car, he decided he was glad tomorrow was Saturday.

So many questions boiled in his mind. Maybe she was right, maybe he did need to give God a chance. But the hard lump of hurt had lodged deep in his heart and it was so hard to let go, to see anything other than Andrea's suffering.

He needed a break from Briony's steady assurance and that solid faith in a God he didn't know. Ten more days of watching over Cristine and she'd be gone.

Ty had no idea how he would manage when Briony left, but he'd figure something out. That was the least of his problems. What bothered him most was that maybe she was right, maybe…

Ty groaned silently. If he was to find his way, he'd have to do it without any help. Hadn't it always been that way?

God expected him to manage, and he would.

As he always had.

For Cristine's sake.

Chapter Eleven

"**I**'m sorry. Did you say immunization?"

Briony pressed the phone tightly against her ear, straining to hear the conversation over Cristine's cantankerous protests.

The voice on the other end explained that Cristine would soon be due for her eighteen-month shot. "She's already behind. She missed her yearly checkup, and we like to keep on top of things."

"I'm just her sitter," Bri explained. "But I'll speak to her father and I'm sure he'll call you back. Can you give me the number again?" She scribbled it down, hung up the phone and glared at Cristine. "I don't like that noise," she told her little charge plainly.

"Neither do I." Ty stood in the doorway, a quirky smile on his handsome face.

Six days later and Briony still couldn't get over it. He was so handsome, so wonderfully kind and gentle. When he wanted to be.

But every day for the past week, he'd also been guarded, restrained and intent on keeping out of her way. Which wasn't easy. Briony often deliberately brushed his shoulder, touched his cheek, squeezed his hand—whatever it took to keep the contact between them going.

He was softening. She could tell.

"What are you doing home?" she asked, lifting Cristine down from her high chair. "We've just finished snack time."

"*We* have? Or Cristine has?"

"Well, actually Cristine. I don't often eat snacks." She couldn't gauge the glint in his eye. "What's up?"

"I just got my promotion." His ear-splitting grin couldn't be suppressed.

"Ty, that's wonderful." Bri threw her arms around his neck and hugged him enthusiastically. "We should celebrate."

She didn't miss the fact that, just for a second, he hugged her back.

"Up, Da," Cristine demanded, and laughed when her father swung her up in the air.

"I thought we'd take that gondola ride you missed. It's a perfect day. There's not a cloud to mar the view."

"Oh, yes. Gondola ride. Uh-huh. Well, that's an idea. We need some fresh air, don't we, Cristine?" She smiled absently when the little girl flapped her arms and kicked her feet.

Bri searched for another topic, then remembered the telephone call and explained. "I could take her in for the shots if you'd like."

"But the doctor's in Calgary." He frowned.

"I know."

"That's a long drive for one person with a baby. What if something happens?" He shook his head. "I wish I'd changed doctors way back when, but Andrea liked this fellow and I just kept taking Cristine there. They have her whole medical history.'' He shrugged. ''Or, at least, as much as we received.''

''Nothing's going to happen, Ty. And if it does, I'll deal with it.'' She smiled to reassure him, love flooding through her as she watched him cradle Cristine. ''Try to trust just a little bit,'' she whispered.

He glanced at her, then the baby. Then he nodded. ''All right, if you're sure you want to. With the holiday season and tourists flooding the place, I could ask for a day off, but I'm not sure I'd get it. We're all on call now.''

''We'll be fine.'' Bri telephoned and made an appointment for Cristine. ''We'll go Friday,'' she told Ty. ''That works out great for me because I'll have some preliminary reports to hand in to Bio-Tek then. It'll be my last day with Cris.''

He ignored her reminder. ''Reports? On what?'' He studied her.

''Oh, a few assessments I've made.'' She began packing a backpack with Cristine's necessities. She guessed he wouldn't give up on the gondola idea. ''I went out hiking again last weekend.''

''Alone?''

She nodded. ''Of course. Overnight this time. It was great.'' She gasped when his fingers closed around her arm. His face was white, taut with strain.

''Don't do it again,'' he ordered.

''Ty—''

''We've had three more bear scares, Briony. You should be traveling in a group. Don't camp alone.''

''All right.'' She felt a shiver of pleasure. He cared! She knew he did, no matter how much he pretended he didn't. "I won't promise to not go, but if I do, I'll phone and tell you first. Fair enough?"

His eyes blazed, but before he could answer the phone rang. He grabbed it. "Hello."

Briony went back to her packing, oblivious to the conversation as she mused on Ty's response.

Please God, keep working on him. He'll come to trust, I know it.

The wonder filled her soul with a glow that would not be quenched.

I love him, God.

"Briony?"

At the touch on her arm, she glanced up.

"It's the minister from that church—First Avenue Fellowship." Ty thrust out the receiver.

Briony felt a flutter of hope grow inside her. *More answers, Lord?*

"Hello, Mr. Winter. Yes, I remember your group." She listened, her heart racing. "Thank you so much for calling. Yes, I certainly will. God bless you, too, sir. Thanks again." She hung up, her fingers clutching the phone number he'd given her.

"Are you going to share whatever is making you stare off into space like that?"

Ty's droll tone penetrated her musing. Briony blinked, focused, then spilled the news.

"One of his group members knew Bridget. This person doesn't mind talking to me, since I'm her sister. She'll be available tonight."

Ty's forehead furrowed. "What more is there to talk about? We already know Cristine's father is dead."

She knew what he was doing, could see it in his eyes. He wanted to avoid the issue, pretend everything was fine. Bri understood that, but she couldn't go along with it. Too many questions lingered in the back of her mind, too many unresolved details. She had to know.

"Maybe it's nothing. Maybe it's something. Either way, I intend to talk to her." She finished stocking the backpack and set it by the door, her mind made up.

"I thought you knew enough. I thought you were prepared to let it go. At last."

The hurt she glimpsed in his eyes almost undid her resolve. But thoughts of Bridget's diary, the heartfelt writing Bri had poured over last night, would not go away.

Briony laid a hand on his arm.

"Try to understand, Ty," she begged. "Bridget loved her baby. I'm positive of that. She knew Peter wasn't coming back and she still wanted the baby. Then one day it all changed and she went searching for adoptive parents. I have to know what made the difference."

"Why?" His eyes were penetrating. "Why hash it through again? She did it, isn't that enough? Why do you have to go snooping through the past?"

Tears pooled in her eyes.

"I'm not deliberately trying to hurt you, Ty. And I would never dream of taking Cristine away. Do you believe me? Will you trust me, about that, at least?" She held his gaze, willing him to see her heart.

At last he nodded. Bri sighed with relief.

"Okay, then. Try to understand. This is my last chance to do something for my sister. I'll be gone soon. I'll be wrapped up in work with no time to go back and reconsider. Before that happens, I want all the information on the table, I want to know every detail." She saw him swallow and knew it was time to beard the lion. "If you were honest with yourself, you'd admit you want to know, too."

He simply stood there, staring at her.

"You're afraid, Ty," she whispered, heart aching to comfort him. "I understand your worry and your fear. But that might be stopping you from gaining some piece of vital information that could help Cristine. Isn't it better to know?"

His lips pinched in a tight line of frustration. "I'm trying to believe what you say. I'm trying to believe God wouldn't kick me when I'm down. But you're asking me to trust blindly, to close my eyes and free-fall."

She watched the hesitation crowd out the fragile thread of trust that had almost surfaced.

"I'm not sure I can do that."

"Oh, Ty, God didn't kick you. He *blessed you* with Cristine! For whatever reason, however He worked it, He sent you a gorgeous daughter. Isn't that proof of His love?"

He didn't answer. Bri knew she had to leave it alone, let God handle it, in his time. Very well, she wouldn't push. But neither would she stop questioning. Surely God had sent her here for just this purpose.

"I guess I'm as ready as I can be, if you are."

He nodded his head once, shook it, then threw up both his hands.

"Yes, I'm ready. No, I'm not! I'll change first. It won't take a minute." He glanced at her light shirt and shook his head. "You need a warm jacket. It's cold up there. And bring a camera. The view is unbeatable."

In fact it took him several minutes, but that gave Briony time to shuffle her sister's diary into her briefcase and snuggle it into a corner of her car where Ty wouldn't be bothered by it.

First, Briony had to go back to the bed-and-breakfast for a warm sweater. Then Ty remembered his video camera, and they trekked back to his place for that.

They didn't leave town until well after six due to the congratulatory phone calls of the other park rangers who teased Ty about his promotion.

"We're later than expected, but at least your mood has improved," Bri teased, as he drove them up the hill through town to the parking lot. She wished the butterflies in her stomach would stop tap dancing.

"They're a nice bunch of guys. It's good to feel like I'm pulling my weight again." He snagged the spot nearest the building and turned to face her. "That's due to you, Briony. If you hadn't come along when you did—"

"God would have sent someone else." She grinned at him cheekily, then climbed out of the Jeep and unfastened Cristine's belt. "Come on, sweetie. We're going way up there." She pointed up the treed slope. "And I hope I don't get dizzy and do something embarrassing."

"Up!" Cristine pointed up the mountain, her eyes shining with excitement.

"That's right, baby. We're going way up there." Briony laughed when Cristine slid her chubby fingers into hers and Ty's. The child frowned at them both.

"What do you want, sweetie?"

"Up!"

They swung her high between them, sharing a smile as Cristine giggled delightedly.

"Up! Up." They kept swinging her until they reached the lower terminal.

"Great! No lineup. We timed this right."

Ty rushed to purchase tickets, while Briony nervously watched another car swing into the terminal.

"Oh, boy," she whispered to Cristine. "I think your auntie needs her head examined."

"Okay, let's go." Ty shepherded them over to the loading area, grinning with delight as the three of them clambered into the gondola car. "We'll climb for eight minutes to the top of Sulphur Mountain, a distance of 2,292 feet. It's a steep track, over five thousand feet long."

"Uh-huh." Bri gulped, then deliberately chose the seat facing the mountain.

As they swung around the cable and left the security of the terminal, the car swayed in a light breeze. Briony sucked in a deep breath and prayed as hard as she could.

"Why don't we switch places?" Ty motioned behind her. "You can't see the panoramic view from there."

"Oh, no! I mean, this is fine," she hissed, her lips pinched together as the gondola dangled in midair, slowly gaining height.

Ty made a motion as if to stand. Bri thrust out her hand. "No! Just stay there. I'm fine. I can see just fine."

He raised his eyebrows. "You've turned a peculiar shade of green," he told her, tongue lodged firmly in one cheek. "Is that normal?"

"Only when I don't have my feet firmly on the ground." Her fingers gripped the seat edge as Cristine danced on the seat beside her, stretching to see everything. Her motion set the car in a rhythmic sway that did strange things to Bri's stomach.

Ty studied Briony's face for a moment longer, then took his daughter and held her so she could see out the windows. "There you go, pumpkin. You can see just fine from here."

"Bee!" Cristine's face crumpled in angry mutiny.

Ty shook his head, his hold tight on her wiggling body.

"Nope. Bee needs some space." He began pointing out the no-doubt fantastic view of the Bow Valley, the peaks of the famous Banff Springs Hotel—anything that would distract Cristine.

Bri kept her eyes front and center. If she bent just a little, peeked out the very top of the window, she could see the treetops falling away underneath them. She made herself relax, inhale, and appreciate the beauty of the forest pressing toward them.

"Oh!" She grabbed the seat again and held on for dear life. "What was that?"

"Just a tower." His eyes darkened in concern. "It bumps a little when we go over some of the supports. Are you all right?"

"No." She took air into her lungs, then grinned. "But I will be. I can see the building." Relief shot through her veins. Soon, please God, her feet would be on solid granite.

"I'm glad you're enjoying it," he commented dryly.

"Oh, I really am." She forced a smile, back teeth clenched tight.

"I can see that." A mocking grin twisted his lips. "You're supposed to glance at the view once or twice, Briony."

"Oh, I will. Later. When I get off this glass-and-metal toy car and stand on a firm foundation."

Bri squeezed her eyes closed for a minute, and held her breath as the car swung up onto the metal support system and into the summit building. Only when they'd finally come to a stop and the attendant had pulled open the door did she exhale.

Ty lifted out Cristine, then held out a hand for Bri, watching as she gingerly stepped onto the cement walkway.

"We could have hiked up, if you'd told me you were afraid of heights," he muttered as he guided them into the visitor complex. "It's primarily switchbacks, but your feet never leave the earth."

"I am not afraid of heights."

He held the door to the outside deck open, his expression carefully blank.

"I enjoyed it." Bri thrust her chin out. "Well, most of it."

He burst out laughing at her grim insistence. "Oh, Briony. Your nose is growing." He shook his head. "What you really enjoyed was getting *out* of the gondola. Admit it."

But Bri was too busy staring over the railing, gaping at the spectacular scene below. "It's gorgeous," she whispered, awe filling her soul. "God has the best view of all."

She felt Ty's eyes on her, but couldn't look away from the vista below. "It's like that old hymn about Mount Pisgah's lofty heights. Look, Ty!" She grabbed his arm, the one that wasn't holding Cristine. "It's like being on top of the world. Those purple-blue mountains seem like a dream. Oh, my, look how the snow glistens such a blazing white on the jagged edges. And the water—did you ever see such turquoise water?"

She couldn't stop gawking.

"I never knew a scientist could wax so poetic." He waited a few minutes, then took her hand and led her toward a metal gate. "Come on, we can hike to Sanson's Peak. It's an old weather station building that's been restored."

Bri exchanged "ohs" with Cristine as they laughed at the mountain sheep that came to explore them during the climb up the steep path in the crisp, cold air.

"I'm glad you told me to bring this sweater," she mumbled as her feet sought a grip among the crumbling bits of granite that littered the trail.

"You're lucky there's no real wind. It can be icy, even in the middle of July."

At last they made it to the hut, where Bri endured Ty's usual photo opportunity. Bri posed the two of them and took a few snaps with her own camera. She had just climbed down off her perch, thanks to Ty's helping hand, when someone tapped her on the shoulder.

"Why don't you go stand with your husband and daughter? I'll take a family picture for you." A woman wearing a toque and mitts smiled generously, her eyes admiring Cristine's blond good looks.

"I'm not—"

"That's a good idea." Ty slipped Bri's camera from around her neck and handed it to the woman. "Where do you think would be a good place?"

Bri couldn't understand what he was doing, why he was pretending that they were a couple, a family, when it wasn't true. Given the number of curious tourists constantly passing them, she had no intention of creating a scene. She simply followed his lead. But her mind swirled with questions.

The woman organized them so that Ty stood behind Briony, his arm around her waist. Cristine stood on the rock beside Bri, her cheeks pink, eyes shining.

"What a gorgeous family!"

Bri heard the comment as a group meandered past them. Her heart clenched at the words. She could no more stop herself from glancing up at Ty than she could stop breathing.

To her amazement, Ty stared back at her, eyes alight with emotions Bri could only guess at. But somewhere underneath, she knew there was love, knew that he cared for her, even though he would never allow himself to say the words.

Oh, Lord, help.

"That's going to make a lovely photo." The woman handed back Bri's camera. "It would make a perfect Christmas card, the two of you gazing into each other's eyes, your daughter clasping her hands like that."

Bri glanced down. Cristine stood beaming up at her, chubby palms together.

"Thank you very much." Ty's voice came out hoarse.

"Oh, you're more than welcome." She beamed a happy smile, stepped back and grabbed her husband's hand. "Do you remember when we were all starry-eyed like them?" She giggled and gave a coy smile as they strolled back to the visitor's center.

"Up." Cristine held up her arm, demanding her father carry her.

"There's a restaurant here. You can sit by the window and look into the valley while you're eating." Ty stared down at Briony, his dark eyes brooding. "We could eat there, unless you're in a rush to get back home.''

''I'd like to share dinner with you,'' she murmured. ''Thank you.''

Who knew what God had in store? Bri wasn't going to miss an opportunity to spend a few more hours with Ty, no matter what the reason.

But as she sat across from him in the circular glass terrace, Bri couldn't help wondering at his thoughts. He listened as she said grace for them all, helped Cristine with her soup and ate his own prime rib, all without looking at her.

''Do you come here often?'' she asked finally. Someone had to say something!

He shook his head. ''Usually just once per season, to watch the mountains change their colors. I don't often work in this area of the park.'' He kept his eyes down.

''I wish you'd tell me what you're thinking,'' Briony burst out, exasperated by his silence. ''If I'd wanted to eat without conversation, I could have come here alone.''

''I was just thinking.'' His eyes flew to hers, offering a glimpse of the emotions warring there, before his lids came down to shutter them.

''About what?'' She pounced on it like a cat on a mouse.

He shrugged. ''Just thinking.''

''About those people believing we're a couple?'' Her cheeks burned at his startled look. ''At how right it felt to pretend, just for a minute, that we really are together? That you care about me as much as I care about you?''

There! She'd said it. Now let him make of it what

he would. Bri stabbed her salmon fillet until it lay scattered in flaky pink bits across her plate. She laid her fork down with a sigh, the hunger draining away.

"I do care about you, Briony." The words seemed torn from him.

"Yes, in your own way, I believe you do." Bri held out Cristine's glass so the little girl could take another drink. "The problem is, you won't admit it to yourself." She held his gaze calmly, her face sad.

"I can't love you, don't you understand? It wouldn't work." The words came out harsh, bitter.

"So you've said." She placed her napkin near her plate. "I'm finished, if you want to leave."

"You don't want to see the sunset from the observation terrace? It's two floors above this."

She pushed back her chair. "By all means, Tyrel, let us visit the observation deck." She looped her camera and her purse around her neck, wiped down Cristine and gathered the little girl into her arms.

"Let's stop by the gift shop, too, and get a souvenir so I can remember my time in Banff. Let's pretend everything is just wonderful."

She turned her back and walked out, hugging Cristine tightly. They spent a few minutes freshening up in the bathroom, then Bri walked back outside. Ty stood waiting for them.

"I'll take her."

Bri turned away. "She's fine. You lead the way."

He sighed, pulled open a door and motioned to the steps. "It's quite a climb."

"Fortunately, I'm not quite dead." She couldn't stop the sarcasm from spilling out.

Hot tears poised, ready to tumble down her cheeks, but Bri gulped them back, stomping up the stairs as if they were the enemy. She ignored Ty as she stepped past him and through the door.

The freshened wind pummeled them as it whistled around the deck, dragging at their clothes, carrying away Ty's comments.

"Pardon?" When he didn't respond, Bri handed him Cristine, who snuggled tightly against his chest for warmth. "If you want to go back, go. I'm going to stay here for a few minutes."

As she walked away from him, the icy wind tore through her thin sweater, biting her skin with the same bitter disregard she attributed to Ty.

"Why, God? Why can't he love me?" Once she knew she was alone, Bri let the tears flow. "Why does the past have to be so important?"

I can never be a father.

The words echoed in her head. She stared out over the verdant valleys with their thick forests and stunning water, and asked herself the question that had hidden in the back of her mind ever since he'd told her the truth.

Even if the impossible happened and Ty somehow agreed to marry her, she would never have a child of her own, never know the thrill of carrying a baby inside her body as Bridget had. She would never know the pains of labor, never feel a tiny mouth nurse at her breast, never watch for the first step.

"It was only ever the slimmest of dreams, anyway," she whispered as the sun drooped down ever lower, nearing the craggy precipices. "I didn't really expect to be a mother any more than I expected to climb those mountains. It was just a dream."

But loving Ty means that dream is dead. It can't happen.

She swallowed as the truth rolled over her in cold waves of implacable fact. Maybe there were treatments available, but even if it were possible, she could never ask Ty to submit to that. She'd seen his face as he talked about the fertility clinic, knew how emasculated he'd felt. He would only end up hating her if she asked him to go through it all again.

"Okay, no baby."

She let the tears flow unchecked as the dream slowly died. The sun slipped a notch in the sky, nearing the rocky horizon. Peace stole upon her in a quiet calm.

"All right, Father. I'll never be a mother. I can learn to live with that. But how can I learn to live without him?"

"Briony?" Ty stood behind her. His hands rested on her waist as he turned her to face him. Cristine sat at his feet, content, for now, to peer through the iron bars.

"Why are you crying?" he whispered, one finger smoothing the tears from her cheeks. "I'm sorry. I didn't mean to make you cry."

She stared up at him, unafraid to let him see all the love that welled up inside. "I love you, Ty. I've never loved anyone like I love you. How can you just ignore that?"

His arms tightened around her, drew her into the warmth of his embrace. "I can't ignore it," he whispered, his lips against her ear. "But I can't accept it, either."

"Why? Just tell me why." It was a cry from the heart. "Do you hate me?"

"God, no!" His mouth pressed against hers in a kiss of desperation, telling her far more than words could ever do.

Bri poured her soul into that kiss. As she did, she begged heaven for help.

"I can't do this to you." Ty drew away suddenly, bent to gather up Cristine, then nestled her in the space between their two bodies, his arm hugging Bri into the circle. Cristine heaved a sigh, laid her head on his chest and closed her eyes.

Bri brushed a curl off the sweet face. "You're not doing anything to me," she whispered. "I love you. And I love Cristine." She dared him to refute it.

"But you've got plans, a career. Your life is ahead of you." He shook his head. "I have nothing to offer."

She tilted up his chin with one finger. "You have the only thing I want," she whispered. "I can change my career, adapt, move."

"How?"

"I don't know! It's a detail, Ty, it can be handled. It was something I pursued so single-mindedly because I had nothing else. It filled a hole I wasn't willing to admit existed. Don't you understand?"

"No." He met her stare. "You spent years pushing for that goal. Are you suddenly going to throw it away, because of me?" He shook his head. "I don't want to be responsible for that."

"You're not." Bri glared at him. "I'm not throwing anything away. I am a scientist. That isn't going to change." She let her fingers slip beneath his collar, cradled the back of his neck.

"I can work anywhere, Ty. As long as the equipment is there, I'll manage."

"But—"

"The only thing I can't do is reorganize my life so I don't love you. It's here—" she pointed to her heart

"—inside me. Part of me. If I wanted to, I couldn't tear it out without tearing out a part of myself."

The wind shifted, brushing past them as if to isolate them in their own little world. Ty stared down at her.

"You tempt me," he whispered as his fingers brushed the golden strands off her face. "This afternoon, when that woman said we were a great family, I wanted to grab that and hang on for all I was worth. I wanted to make the dream reality."

"So why don't you?" she coaxed. "Why can't you accept that I love you and Cristine, that I want to be part of your lives?"

One finger traced her bottom lip.

"You'll always be part of our lives, Briony." He rested his chin on Cristine's head. "But I can't let you give up your whole life for something that could change at any moment."

She frowned. "What are you talking about?"

"I have this terrible fear, Briony. Apprehension, terror. Call it whatever you will." He bowed his head, his forehead pressing against hers. "For a very long time I've tried to pretend that Cristine's adoption was perfectly ordinary."

His daughter shifted in his arms. He glanced down, his face glowing with tenderness and love that Bri could see included her, too.

When Ty finally spoke, one lonely tear hung suspended from the end of his long dark lashes. "The truth is, I fell in love with Cristine that very first day. I refused to believe there was anything wrong, anything strange in Andrea's sudden silences or the way she avoided answering me."

"Oh, Ty." Love squeezed her heart.

"When Andrea died, the fear multiplied. I ignored

the truth about Andrea, pretended everything was all right when it wasn't. Then she died. In the back of my mind, I always wondered when God would make me face the reality about Cristine." He took a deep breath.

"That's why I don't want you to contact that woman from the fellowship group, that's why I didn't want to ever find Cristine's biological father, and that's why I can't let myself love you." The white lines radiating around his mouth testified to his dread.

"I always lose the thing that matters most, Briony. It's only a question of when. Losing Cristine will be hard enough, when the time comes. I can't—I won't—let myself fall in love with you, only to lose you, too."

Briony stood there with her arms around him and knew there was nothing she could do, nothing she could say. God would have to handle it.

"I love you, Ty," she whispered, as they stood watching the sun dip behind the mountains in a wash of baby-soft pink. "I'll keep on telling you that until the day that I die, but I think it's something you'll have to trust in."

His shoulders slumped. The tender-soft eyes dulled, lost their chocolate glow. Her heart winced at the haggard fear washing over his beloved face.

"I don't have any faith left, Briony. I'm sorry."

Ty's words were carried away on the wind, their plaintive sound tearing at her insides. She watched him turn and walk away from her, cradling Cristine, the last of his hopes and dreams for the future, against his chest with heartbreaking tenderness.

"Then, I'll have to have enough faith for both of us, my darling," she murmured as she walked to the stairs, climbed down to the main deck and followed him out to the little cars waiting to carry them down the mountain.

But later, as Ty drove them back to his cottage, the foreboding he'd only mentioned followed like a specter.

It was only a matter of time until the truth came out.

And only God could control what happened after that.

Chapter Twelve

Ty stonewalled that dreaded phone call with every possible means he could find to delay the truth.

But once Cristine had been bathed and put to bed, once he'd re-tidied the immaculate kitchen Briony always left, once he'd brewed a pot of coffee and poured some for both of them, there was nothing more to do.

"You might as well go ahead and call her."

And thus Ty gave Briony permission to start the nightmare he knew would end in grief.

He sat in his living room with his hands clasped between his knees, watching as Briony punched in the number. His senses screamed at him, ordering him to get out while he could, to refuse to let her call, to send her away. His mind told him he was a fool to dance so close to the edge. His heart told him that the truth would come out eventually.

It was time to face the music.

If he could have, Ty would have prayed. As it was, he sat numb, cold, immobilized by dread he couldn't explain.

Bri switched to the speakerphone. Ty tensed as a woman's voice answered on the fourth ring.

Oh, God, please...

Please what? Make it go away?

"Mrs. King? My name is Briony Green. I believe you knew my sister, Bridget?"

Too late for that now.

Ty sat frozen as Bri explained how she had found the fellowship group, had read her sister's diary, was trying to understand what Bridget had been going through almost two years ago.

"Yes, indeed! I met her just after she learned her boyfriend had died. She was very confused." Mrs. King's confident voice left little room for doubt. "I became quite friendly with her, though I must say, I had no idea Bridget had family. Other than Will, of course. He was her rock and she loved him dearly."

"Will? Oh, Peter. Yes, we've just recently learned about him."

"So tragic when he died. Poor Bridget didn't know what to do. I think that's what drew me to her, made me want to help her. She wanted that baby so desperately, but she knew she couldn't raise it. She'd been told she had a very serious disease. Her pregnancy meant she couldn't seek treatment because the medication would impact the baby." Mrs. King tut-tutted. "Terrible thing. She wanted so badly to believe she would recover, but she was also afraid she wouldn't."

Ty hadn't known about the disease, but it was obvious Briony had. She simply kept plying the woman with questions, her scientist's mind absorbing the facts in neat, precise order.

"You got to know Bridget quite well?"

"As I say, we were friendly for the first few meetings. Four, I think."

"Then what happened?"

Ty closed his eyes.

A sour note crept into Mrs. King's voice. "A woman named Andrea started attending. After the first meeting, those two were like peas in a pod. Then it seemed Bridget wanted to speak only to her. I didn't like to interfere."

Ty wanted to be anywhere but here. He could just imagine his wife's envy of Bridget's pregnancy, her constant hovering, her whispered comments about single mothers. He opened his eyes and faced reality, whatever it might be.

"I'm sorry, I don't understand." Bri frowned at the phone, her eyes moving to Ty. "Why was Andrea there?"

"Something about her nerves, I think. We don't always give exact reasons. It's more just a venue to share if you want." She coughed lightly. "I was having a bit of a rough go myself. Perhaps I didn't always pay a lot of attention to Andrea's ranting. I'm afraid I mostly avoided her."

"I see."

Andrea's ranting. Bri's disappointment touched him all the way across the room. He knew she'd expected more concrete information, something specific.

Ty fumed at his own inadequacy. He couldn't help her now. He hadn't even known Andrea was attending a group.

"My dear, it was obvious to me that Andrea needed more than we could give. She needed professional care. She had these mood swings. Sometimes you could talk her out of them, sometimes not.'' Mrs. King sighed.

''Please continue.''

''Up, down. Up, down. I felt sorry for the woman's family, I'll tell you. Five minutes after meeting Bridget, *zip,* her mood was sky high! It was very hard to deal with. You never knew when she was going to blow.''

''I understand.'' Bri chewed her bottom lip, her fingers busy scribbling notes on the white pad in front of her. She swung her legs up underneath her and hunkered over the phone. ''Do you happen to know when or why Bridget decided to give her baby up for adoption?''

''Of course I know! I remember the afternoon well. Someone mentioned that their daughter was driving them nuts and they were thinking about boarding school.'' Mrs. King chuckled. ''My dear, we all had problems with our kids at that time.''

Silence stretched, yawned and finally snapped.

''But our Miss Andrea stood up and said that people who had problems raising children shouldn't be allowed to have them, that they were too self-centered to devote themselves to their children's needs instead of their own pursuits.''

''But what about my sister?''

''The very next week Bridget announced that she was going to give her baby up for adoption.''

''I see.''

Ty leaned forward. Time to clear the air.

''Mrs. King, I'm the person who adopted Bridget's baby. My name is Ty Demens.''

''Oh, you're Andrea's husband.'' Stern disapproval clouded the formerly friendly voice.

"Yes, I am. Did the entire group know that Andrea was to be the baby's new mother?"

"Oh, no. Bridget took me aside one night and told me she was having second thoughts about the adoption. She wondered if Andrea's hus—er, if the baby would have a good home."

Embarrassment and anger raged inside, but Ty choked it down. He *had* to know. "Did she say why?"

Silence.

"Please, Mrs. King, we really need to know. You can be frank." Ty gritted his teeth and waited.

"Well, it was just that from the stories, I guess Bridget wasn't sure how suitable he—you would be. I'd really rather not relate what she said. Everything is supposed to be in confidence, you know."

Bri's commiserating eyes told Ty she knew how much the words stung him. What on earth had Andrea intimated?

"I can reassure you, Mrs. King, that Ty is the best possible father any little girl could ever have."

"Oh." A sigh of relief. "That's all right, then."

"Could you please tell us some of what Andrea said? Specifically?" said Bri.

"Well, it's rather personal."

Ha! Ty stifled the ready response. His character, his personality, his beliefs had been discussed in that room, and she was afraid it was *rather personal?*

"We have to know so that we can understand several things that have happened since. Please tell us." He waited.

"Andrea wanted a family. We all knew that. I gathered that there was some, er, problem. On your part."

He winced at the baldness of it.

"Andrea said you refused to consider any of the

new things the doctors can do these days. She said you seemed perfectly happy to go on as things were, but that her heart was breaking to have a baby.'' The woman's starched tones softened.

"We could see that for ourselves. She doted on children, fawned over several other ladies' wee ones. When she was with them, her moods were gone and she was a different person. That's partly why I agreed to convince Bridget.''

"Convince?'' Ty sat up straight, every nerve in his body on red alert. "I thought she *wanted* to give up the baby.''

"She did. She did! Bridget was just confused. I reminded her that Andrea had a settled home, a marriage that seemed fairly stable. Andrea said you—they'd discussed adoption and that her husband was agreeable, so I convinced Bridget she'd made the right decision.''

Bri's quiet voice broke in. "When did this conversation take place, Mrs. King?''

"Oh, we had variations on it several times. But the last time Bridget got really upset was when she was in labor. She kept saying she'd have to see the baby first, hold her, then decide.'' Mrs. King sniffed. "Well, I just didn't see the sense in her fussing over that while she was dealing with labor pains. Besides, everything had already been arranged.''

"Arranged?'' Ty couldn't believe what he was hearing.

"Why, yes. Andrea had the papers all drawn up ahead of time. In fact, I believe you'd signed them that very morning. I witnessed the signatures of the others. Andrea said everything had to be signed and sealed, a done deal, or her husband wouldn't allow it. I thought it a mite callous to rush everything through like that, but Andrea was so desperate.''

She didn't say anything for a minute, as if only then realizing to whom she was speaking.

"Go on." Ty didn't know how he choked the words out. Anger burned inside with a deep, penetrating grief. Why had Andrea done it? Why?

"You have no idea how nervous I was when they left for Calgary that afternoon. Mercy, the poor girl was already in labor! I could only hope and pray they made it safely.''

"Why didn't my sister have the baby here?" Briony's pale face looked lost, forlorn. Ty watched her fingers snap the pencil she held into two pieces.

"Oh, honey, Banff is far too small for that. Everyone would know about it, wouldn't they." She tut-tutted. "No, it was better to be in Calgary. If anything happened, the facilities were right there. Besides, Andrea had a nice little hotel room all arranged for Bridget after she got out of the hospital."

Ty cast his mind back, remembering the credit card statements he'd questioned and Andrea's glib answer that she'd had to be near the lawyer's office while the adoption process was negotiated. A sour taste filled his mouth.

"She was such a smart woman, so organized." Admiration shone through her words. "Do you know, Andrea even phoned the hotel and told them Bridget had been rushed to the hospital and wouldn't be in to work for three weeks?"

"No, I didn't know that." Bri's voice barely carried. Her face shone wet with tears.

Ty couldn't stand it any longer; he got up and moved to sit beside Briony. He wrapped his arm around her shoulder and hugged her close, wishing he could take away some of the pain she must be feeling.

"They named her Cristine. That was the one thing Bridget insisted on. We never knew why—she never said." A soft sigh washed over the line. "She was such a darling child, so pretty. Newborns often aren't, you know."

Ty swallowed the bile that rose in his throat. "You—saw the new baby?"

"Of course. The very night she was born. Andrea insisted the child spend her first night in her very own home. The doctors found nothing wrong, and besides, there was an awful pileup from that snowstorm the day before. Remember? They needed every bed."

Briony's hands were icy cold as they grabbed at Ty, her face a stark gray-white.

"Did Bridget ever see her baby?" she whispered, her fingers clutching Ty's. "Did she get to hold her at least once?"

"Oh, yes. They'd agreed that Bridget could hold the child after she gave birth. But that was the only time."

"And my sister was happy with that?"

Ty's heart ached for the pain in her voice, shadowing her eyes. It hurt to know he'd been a part of it.

"Why, I believe so, dear. She made the deal, after all."

The careless words bit at Ty. "Did she know that she had a period of grace? That she could change her mind if she wanted?"

"I don't know." Mrs. King's voice came across the line less assured now. "Andrea dropped out of our group after that. Well, she had to, with the baby and all. And, of course, Bridget never came back. She transferred out of the hotel a short time later, I understood.''

His mind screamed. Why had God done this? Why such misery, such pain?

''And you never saw her again?'' Ty had to ask it, had to force out the question he knew Briony longed to ask, but to which she couldn't bear to hear the answer.

''I didn't see Andrea again. Someone told me she'd passed away. But now that you mention it, I did see Bridget again. I'd almost forgotten.'' Mrs. King's voice softened. ''The end of that summer, as I recall. She was standing at the corner of Bear Street.''

''Doing what?''

''Nothing. Just standing there. Staring at a house. Then she turned around and left. That's the last time I saw her.''

Briony gulped, then nodded, her face awash with tears. ''Thank you, Mrs. King. Thanks for all your help.''

''I'm sure you're welcome as can be. I hope I haven't said anything out of turn.''

''Don't worry about it.'' Ty added his thanks, then punched the speaker button off with a vicious jab. ''I should have known,'' he groaned. He jumped to his feet and paced the room, filled with impotent rage that would not be quieted.

He couldn't stand to watch the grief and loss overwhelm Briony, couldn't bear to see the agony tear her apart. Neither could he bear to face the truth.

''I'm not her father,'' he whispered at last, staring at Briony as he admitted the truth. ''She was never mine. Andrea committed a terrible sin by taking her.''

He flopped into his chair, head in his hands. ''I

should have known. I should have guessed that's why she was so secretive. Why didn't I question her more, demand to know all the answers? Why didn't I force the issue?''

''It wouldn't have mattered. Bridget knew what she was doing.'' Bri's voice sounded ragged, distorted. ''I'm certain she did what she felt best.''

He jerked his head up, glared at her. ''After having just given birth?'' he demanded, shocked that even now she refused to lay blame. ''You really believe she understood that she would never see her child again when my wife ripped her baby out of her arms and carried Cristine away?'' He snorted in disgust.

''Ty, we don't know exactly what happened.''

He shook his head, eyes bitter as he watched the tears form white tracks down her cheeks.

''I know, Briony. I know exactly what my wife would have done under those circumstances, given the slimmest chance for adoption.'' He groaned, only then assimilating the whole truth.

''And I was a party to it. I let it go because I was too cowardly to demand answers.''

Every bone, every muscle, every nerve in his body ached as the truth washed over him in a tidal wave of pain. God was stripping away the last thing he cared about—his beloved child.

He'd lost it all—Cristine had never really been his.

''She's not my daughter,'' he whispered, speaking the truth he'd always sensed deep inside. ''What Andrea did, what she coerced your sister into doing, was terribly wrong. Cristine should have been your child, Briony. You should be raising her. Not me.''

Briony's blond head lifted. Her eyes widened, darkened as she stared at him. ''What?''

"You have to take her, Briony. I have no right to deprive you of that child. She isn't mine. She never really was. My life with her is based on trickery and deceit. She should never have borne my name. I just got to look after her for a while."

"Ty, no!" Bri couldn't believe what she was hearing. She surged to her feet, her fists clenched at her sides.

"You listen to me, Tyrel Demens, and you listen hard." She squatted in front of him, her face mere inches from his. "Don't you tell me Cristine's being here is a lie. Don't you dare say it's a mistake!"

She picked up his hand and held it tightly between hers. "Maybe it didn't happen as we would have liked, but God knew exactly what he was doing. He placed my niece in a home where no one—" she met his gaze head-on, her eyes blazing "—and I do mean *no one* could have loved her more. I believe Bridget knew what she was doing. She believed God's perfect plan was for Cristine to be with you."

"But—"

"There was no mistake, Ty. Not one. I think God led her to Andrea because he knew your love would make up for anything else Cristine lacked in her life."

"I do love her." Ty nodded, his eyes glassy. "That's why I'm turning her over to you. I love Cristine enough to do the right thing for her."

Bri peered up at him. "What do you mean, *the right thing?*"

"You're the person she should be with, Briony. You're strong and courageous, you keep pushing until you find the truth. You don't have any horrible shameful actions in your past. You're open and honest.

You'll make Cristine a wonderful mother." His face was closed up like a mask, hiding his emotions.

She stared at him, unable to believe what she was hearing. "What are you saying, Ty? You mean you love me? You want us to be a family?"

His sad eyes shimmered with tears he refused to shed.

"I can't love you, Briony. With every fiber of my being I long to, but it wouldn't work." He smiled gently. "I ruin everything I touch. I get so self-involved, I drive people to do the wrong thing. I've offended God, and he's taking away what I most want."

"That's foolishness, Ty."

He shook his head, his eyes deadly serious. "No, it's the cold hard truth that I've avoided for too long."

"But I told you, I explained—" She stopped when he held up a hand.

"You have a wonderful faith, Briony. Don't let anyone ever spoil that." His voice dropped to a whisper. "I envy you that unfaltering confidence. But it's not for me. It just doesn't work for me."

Tears poured down her face. "It could," she whispered, praying he'd understand.

Ty shook his head. "No," he said. "You're so full of love. Once you let yourself step out of the cocoon you build around yourself, you'll find yourself longing to share that love with a family." He squeezed his eyes closed.

"I can't give you children, Briony. No matter how much I want to, it's not possible. God knows, if I could I would do anything to alter that, but it will never change. And I won't make the same mistake twice."

"What mistake? Andrea's problems were not your

fault, Ty.'' She prayed as she spoke, begging the Father of all children to heal the hurt she saw shining in Ty's eyes.

''Weren't they?'' He shook his head. ''You can't erase the guilt, Briony. You can't change the truth. Twice in my life I've ignored someone else's needs and it's cost them dearly. I will not repeat my mistake, especially not with you.''

He bent toward her, brushed his lips across her eyelids and smiled. ''Please don't cry, my darling. This one unselfish thing I'm doing is for you.''

Bri pulled back, worried by the tone of his voice. Desperately she searched his face for answers.

''What, exactly, are you doing, Ty?''

''I'm giving you Cristine.'' His voice wobbled, broke. He forced a rigid control on himself.

''I don't understand. How can you give me Cristine?'' Bri couldn't fathom the funny-sad little smile that touched his lips, couldn't discern the meaning that glimmered in the depths of his dark chocolate eyes.

''Please. Just tell me what you're saying.''

He stood then, straightened his shoulders like a soldier preparing for battle. His hands dropped to his sides, his chin thrust upward.

''I'm having the adoption nullified. You will be Cristine's mother. You are the rightful parent.''

Bri gasped, horror filling her soul with panic. ''No!''

Oh, Father, what have I done? What damage has my poking and probing inflicted?

Tyrel nodded, eyes hard. Cold. ''Yes. It's only proper that Cristine be raised as your child. I have no right, no claim to her. I will never be her father.''

There was something wrong here, something she

didn't understand. Ty's self-blame came from something in the past. Bri knew she had to find out what it was. Sometime. Not now.

Now Briony wanted to rail at him, to scream her denial until he took back what he'd said. Of course he was Cristine's father! How could he ever deny it?

But the outrage blocked her throat, as a strangled cry jangled around the silent room from the baby monitor sitting on a side table.

"Cristine!" Ty spun toward the stairs and raced up the risers three at a time.

Bri followed him, her feet less nimble, her mind still rejecting his words. When she arrived in Cristine's room, the little girl was sitting up in bed coughing desperately, fighting to draw another breath. Ty's big hands tried to soothe her.

"What's the matter?"

He turned tortured eyes toward Bri, the brown orbs brimming with stomach-clenching fear.

"He's taking her away," he whispered, as Cristine gasped beneath his hand. "I told you, I mess up and God takes away everything I love. It's a punishment."

"Stop it!"

Bri knew nothing about medicine, even less about childhood diseases, but she knew God, and she knew He did not punish innocent children for the error of someone else's ways.

With energy born of desperation, she shoved Ty out of the way and assessed the situation. Cristine was choking. Briony didn't know how or why she knew that, she just knew.

"God, please help me now," she whispered, then she swabbed the baby's mouth with a damp washcloth, searching for something, anything that would ease Cristine's breathing.

Ty's whitened face sought reassurance. "Her color's returning a little. Isn't it?"

Briony grabbed a couple of blankets, wrapped them around the beloved body and snatched Cristine into her arms.

"We have to get her to the hospital, Ty."

He stood there, paralyzed by the fear that consumed him.

"I love her so much," he whispered, eyes almost black in his pale face. "But He's taking her, anyway."

"Ty!" She grabbed his arm, jerked it hard. "I'm taking her to the hospital. Either help or get out of the way."

He looked at her dazed, then glanced down as Cristine cried out. She help up her arms, wiggling in Briony's embrace, begging for her daddy to carry her.

"Are you going to abandon your daughter now?" Bri whispered.

Without a word, Ty grabbed the little girl into his arms and left the room. Bri followed him down, joy filling her soul as quickly as the worry.

Okay, God, she prayed silently as she drove the Jeep toward the hospital. *You've got something wonderful planned here. Help me to be a part of it. Whatever it is, whatever it costs, let me help Ty to find you.*

She drove through the town as fast as she dared, weaving in and out of the evening traffic. Ty directed her, and within minutes she was able to pull up at the emergency entrance.

As she followed Ty into the building, Bri's nonstop prayer continued.

I love Ty, you know that. But if I can't have him or

Cristine, please take care of them for me. Please show Ty that Your plans don't include taking away everything he loves.

As she dashed into the first cubicle, Briony caught the doctor's low-spoken reaction.

"It might be meningitis."

"Oh, God!"

Her eyes met Ty's.

"Faith," she whispered. "Just a little bit of faith, Ty. Like a grain of sand. Trust him. What have you got to lose?"

"Everything."

Chapter Thirteen

"**Y**ou'll have to leave. Now. You're only impeding our work." The nurse held the door open, waiting.

Though Ty resisted the tug on his arm, Briony pulled even harder, until, finally, he followed.

"Come on, we'll go out on the patio."

"But Cristine—"

"Is in the best hands she could be in. They'll find us if anything changes."

He followed Bri through the small hospital. When they reached the red-bricked patio, she pressed him down onto a bench, grasped his hands in hers and began praying out loud, pouring her heart out to the only One who could heal the entire mess.

After a while a nurse brought them each a glass of orange juice. The doctors were still working on Cristine. There was no change and no firm diagnosis. Bri slipped out of the room long enough to dial Clarissa's number and ask her to pray.

"It's bad, Clarissa. And it's more than Cristine's illness. Get Blair to pray, too, will you?"

"Of course. Heaven's gates will be flooded, honey."

"Thanks."

"Briony?"

"Yes?"

"Is he the one?"

Bri swallowed, her mind brimming with all the reasons Tyrel Demens believed he couldn't let her into his life. But then the peace of God, the assurance of His love, swept into her heart.

"Yes, Clarissa. He's the one. God willing."

"I believe God's willing, honey. Otherwise He wouldn't have led you there in the first place. Go to him now. I'll get Blair and we'll start praying."

"I love you."

"I know." Clarissa laughed gently, her voice soft with reassurance. "I love you, too, Bri. I still expect to be invited to your wedding."

"From your lips to God's ear." Bri hung up the phone and hurried back to Ty.

He sat staring at the water that spilled quietly into the fountain. His eyes seemed riveted on the flood of light that shone down on a small cement sculpture of a shepherd with a sheep cuddled in his arms.

"It reminds me of Cristine," he whispered, when Bri slipped into the seat beside him. "Only He's doing a better job than I ever could." His fingers knotted.

"Ty, I need some answers." It was time for the whole truth. Bri swallowed and plunged ahead.

"Why do you feel so guilty? Why do you think it's your fault, that bad things have happened because of something you did? What *two* things were you talking about?"

"Things happened because I didn't measure up. Not ever." The words came out coldly unemotional.

"I don't understand that." She waited patiently, praying as she did.

"I don't want to talk about this."

She took his face in her hands and forced him to see her. "We have to talk about it. Now. Tell me."

After a moment, he nodded.

"Andrea died because of the strain of having Cristine around. She should never have had to deal with that. If I'd been doing my job as her husband, if I'd stuck to my guns and looked after her interests by refusing to consider adoption, she might still be alive."

A derisive smile tugged at his mouth. "But no, I made my own life easier by going along with this adoption, quelled my own conscience when I knew there was something wrong. That's what killed my wife. Me."

Bri thought for a minute. "Andrea might be alive today, but would she have been happy without Cristine in her life?"

He frowned, tilted his head and looked at her.

"She wouldn't, would she? She craved a baby, longed for a child. Cristine must have been everything she dreamed of."

"And a lot more, besides." He shook his head, his eyes straying to the past. "She was up all the time, worried silly that she'd do something wrong. Neither of us slept much, but she hardly slept at all. She said it was her only chance to be a mother and she couldn't miss anything."

"She loved Cristine."

"Uh-huh."

"That's what matters, don't you see?" She laid her

palm against his jaw and turned his face toward her. "God doesn't expect perfect people. He expects people who love Him and do their best. He can manage all the rest on His own."

"But I should have—"

She put her finger to his lips. "Answer me honestly, Ty. Did you love Andrea?"

"Yes, but—"

"Good. Do you love Cristine?"

His eyes darkened, his mouth trembled. "Yes."

The firm clear ring of those words gave her courage. "Do you love me?"

It took him a long time, but he finally exhaled and nodded. "Yes."

Bri couldn't believe he'd said it so casually. "That's it? That's all you're going to say?"

"No." He pulled her into his arms, kissed her, then spoke.

"Sometimes, like today on the mountain, I let myself think what it would be like if we were a family, if I could wake up every morning and see your gorgeous hair spread across the pillow. I daydream about Christmas together, in front of the fire, about Cristine playing with Giselle's new baby." His hands trembled as they touched each feature on her face.

"It's like a mirage, Briony, shimmering in front of me, too beautiful to be true. Just for a moment, for a tiny second, I'm tempted to reach out and grab it."

"And then?"

"Then I realize what kind of a life that would be for you." His hand smoothed her hair. "You once told me your secret desire was for a baby. You couldn't have that with me, Bri. Not ever."

"But—"

It was his turn to silence her, one lean finger stopping the words.

"Listen to me, my darling. Please?"

She nodded.

"At first you'd say it wouldn't matter. You'd put a brave face on, try to compensate in a thousand different ways. But it would eat away at you, you'd start to look around you at other women who were having babies and you'd realize that you'd made a mistake. You'd want out."

Bri shoved him away, fury building inside. "Stop it, Ty!"

"What did I do?" His shocked gaze met her angry one.

Fighting for control, Bri prayed for patience.

"Before you were married, Ty, before you knew you couldn't have children, did you look at every woman you saw and rate her on whether or not she would make a good birthing machine?"

"Of course not." His face reddened, his eyes shone with hurt. "That's horrible."

"Suppose it was me, then. Just suppose I could never have children. Would that stop you from marrying me, from loving me, from caring about me?"

"No." He wrapped his arms around her and hugged her close. "I care for you because of who you are, not because of what you could or couldn't give me. God help me, I love you."

Tears welled in her eyes. "Don't you see? It's the same with me. I love you because you're you, warts and all." She kissed his nose.

"Thousands of people marry and then find out they will never be parents. They marry because they love each other, because they want to be together. That's the prerequisite for marriage. And we've got it because God brought us together.''

He hugged her tightly for a minute, then frowned. ''But I failed Cristine. Now God will take her away, too.'' His hands shook as they held her.

''You're making me very angry with this illogical argument,'' she told him pertly. ''Would you please explain how you failed Cristine? Don't you love her?''

''Of course.'' His eyes glowed.

''Don't you care for her, meet every possible need, give her the very best you can no matter what it costs you?''

''I try.''

''Well, then, you and God have something in common because that's exactly what He does for you. Only He does it a lot better.''

At last Ty spoke the fear that had lain buried in his heart for too long. ''But what if He takes her away from me?''

''My darling Ty, God would only do that for a very, very good reason. And all your fussing and arguing and worrying won't change His plan one iota.'' She combed her hands through his hair.

''He brought her to you when she needed someone strong who could survive when her mommy died, He blessed you with her bubbly life and joy, He made sure you were the kind of man who didn't think it was foolish to care for a tiny baby when other men were out with the guys.''

Bri shook her head, daring him to contradict her. ''I love you, Tyrel Demens, but you're making me crazy with this ridiculous fear. God went to great pains to choose a wonderful daddy for Cristine because He loves her even more than you do.''

He shifted uncomfortably, but Bri wouldn't let up.

"Are you now telling me God messed up when He picked you? Are you telling me you're not up to the challenge, that you think your plan is better than His?"

"Well, when you put it like that—I guess not." He smiled sheepishly.

"Well, hallelujah! A light at last." She'd pressed this far, but something still eluded her. "Who was the second person you said you let down?"

His face froze.

"I have to know." She sat and waited for him to empty himself of all the pain.

A sigh shuddered through him.

"He was my friend, my partner. We were on a rescue together." The flat hard tone offered the facts in cold, brisk precision. "Some hikers got lost in a blizzard. We were assigned to bring them out."

"And this friend of yours got hurt?" It was beginning to make sense. Bri covered his hand with her own. "Just tell me, okay, Ty?"

"It was rough, really rough. He wanted to go around, take an easier route. I was worried about the hikers suffering from exposure. I insisted we do it my way, march straight in and bring them out. It had to be my way. I knew best. I always know best."

The self-condemnation in his words tugged at Bri's soft heart. How long had he carried this burden?

"What happened?"

"I pushed him too hard. He was tired, needed a break. I said we'd take one when we got across the river." Ty's voice broke, then resumed, rough, intense. "He never made it."

"I'm sorry."

"One minute he was there, telling me to slow down.

The next he was slipping away. He fell.'' He stopped, took a deep breath and continued. ''The current was too fast. I couldn't reach him, and he couldn't reach my rope. Three days later they found his body six miles downstream.''

''And the hikers?''

''I got them out, all of them. They were fine, no problem. They had enough provisions that they could have lasted at least another day. Certainly, fifteen or twenty minutes of rest time wouldn't have made a difference. I just had to have my own way. I had to be in charge.'' He turned to look at her.

''When Andrea's depression got worse, I decided I would never push her as I had him. I'd let her find her own solutions, see the doctors she wanted. If she asked, I went. If she didn't, I let her handle it. I figured that later, once she realized there wasn't going to be a baby in our immediate future, she'd settle down, find another interest.''

''There was nothing wrong with that.''

He smiled sadly. ''Wasn't there? I was jealous, Bri. Jealous that a baby would take my place with her. I wanted to be the center of her world, I wanted us to be strong together, like a team. I gave her all the love I had, and it fell short. I didn't do enough.''

''She was sick, Ty.''

He nodded, his eyes slipping back to focus on the shepherd. ''I know. I knew it then, too. But that didn't make it any easier to take. I wouldn't take more tests, pretend it could be changed, trail around to doctor after doctor. I knew it was hopeless and I refused to do things her way. I drove her to it, Briony. Because I was so stubborn, she found a way to get her beloved baby.''

Bri didn't know what to say.

"When Andrea died, I realized Cristine was my last chance. I couldn't mess up again, I had to get it right. I think I knew He'd take her, too. I just didn't know when." The lines around his eyes deepened. "I never told another soul, never let anyone even see what I knew. But it was always there, hidden away in a place I wouldn't have to look, to see my own culpability."

"Ty, you were not in control." How could she make him see? "You didn't know how Andrea got Cristine. I'm not sure we know even yet. Maybe that's the way it's supposed to be. Maybe it's a mystery we will only know when we get to heaven."

His lips pinched together. "It isn't enough."

She smiled. "It has to be. I haven't quite finished Bridget's diary, but I've read enough to know that she was all right with her decision. She felt she'd done what God wanted her to do and she was ready to go on to face her illness." The certainty filled her heart, calmed her soul, gave her strength to meet his painful gaze.

"That's exactly what we have to do now. We have to face Cristine's illness with faith and trust that somehow, behind all the mystery and confusion, there is a reason. There is a plan."

Like a tonic, Bri felt God's assurance healing her. "Bridget was led to Banff, led to Andrea. She didn't get hoodwinked, she trusted in her Father and believed He knew what He was doing." She hugged him.

"And boy, did He! Cristine got a loving father, Ty. She got a daddy handpicked from heaven itself."

"But I'm not really—"

She placed a finger across his lips.

"Don't say it again," she told him firmly. "You're

demeaning what God planned when you try to change His way. Don't you think the God of the universe could have brought Bridget home to me if He'd wanted me to have Cristine? Don't you think His master mind could have found a way, if that's what He intended?"

Ty frowned, then slowly nodded. "Maybe. I guess."

"Don't you see, my darling man? God took what could have been a bad situation, and He turned it into something fantastic. He introduced us through Cristine, and then made it possible for me to stay around long enough for my heart to be filled with love for you."

Finally Ty relented, moved by the tenderness in her voice. His arm crept around her shoulder, hugging her close to his body as the wonder of it filled his mind.

"Next, you'll be claiming He helped my mother trip," he murmured, eyes bright with hope.

Bri shook her head, her face warm with love. "No, but I do think He used that. He knew I only had a month here, so He worked fast." She grinned.

Ty kissed her nose, then frowned. "What about your job, Bri?"

She waved a hand. "He can work that out, too. I don't see why I should spend my time second-guessing Him."

"That faith of yours!" Ty shook his head in wonder. "I'm beginning to believe your faith could move those mountains out there."

She smiled. "It all starts with trust, Ty. Once He's got your trust, He can do anything."

"You're sure that you won't accept my offer, you won't be Cristine's mother?"

Bri shook her head slowly. "No, Ty. There's only

one way I could ever be a mother to Cristine, and you know it.''

He leaned forward and kissed her nose again, his eyes dark with emotion. His fingers squeezed hers in a promise that echoed in the depth of his eyes.

"One miracle at a time, Briony. Let's concentrate on one miracle at a time."

"Cristine is going to be fine. God has big plans for her."

The words had no sooner left her mouth than a nurse hurried toward them. "The doctor says you can sit with her for a while."

Ty's eyes flickered with hope. "She's better?"

"No change. Not yet." The nurse turned, motioned to the door. "Please come."

Bri followed them to Cristine's bed, but she stopped Ty outside the door. "Faith and trust, Ty. They open the door to God and allow Him to show the way."

He grinned halfheartedly as his fingers laced through hers. "I'm trying to see that, Bri. I've had a wonderful fifteen months with that little girl. If that's all I get, I'll try to be glad." His mouth trembled for a minute, but he regained his control. "Will you pray with me, help me ask God for the ability to accept His decision? Whatever it is."

She stood on her tiptoes and brushed his cheek with her lips. "I'd love to pray with you."

They sat by the bed praying, sometimes aloud, sometimes silently. The dark night stretched endlessly on until Bri could keep her eyes open no longer. Though nothing had changed in Cristine's condition, though the labored breathing and tortured coughs still continued, Bri's assurance never wavered.

"This is a test, Ty," she murmured as her head

drooped against his shoulder, her eyes too heavy to open. "Will we trust or will we lean unto our own understanding?"

He held her close, head bent. Just before she drifted off, Bri heard him repeat a scripture she vaguely remembered.

"Before they call, I will answer."

The answer was on the way, she just had to wait.

"Briony?" A light kiss brushed across her cheek as a muscular arm shook her gently awake. "Bri?"

"What?" She forced her lids up and peered at him.

"Someone wants to say 'good morning.'"

Bri surged forward, her eyes flying to the small body still lying in the bed. Cristine's big blue eyes were wide open and sparkling with life. Though her face was still a little warm, she exhibited none of the lethargy from the night before.

"Hello, darling," Bri whispered. "Auntie Bri is so glad to see you smile."

"Bee." Cristine's eyes fluttered for a moment, then drooped closed.

"She'll sleep a lot today, but she's definitely on the mend."

"What was it?" Ty's voice almost broke, but he kept his eyes on the doctor and his arm firmly wrapped around Briony.

The doctor shook his head. "I'm not sure if we'll ever know. We see this sometimes—a viral infection that takes over, then disappears. There's no rhyme nor reason to either the illness or the cure." He shrugged, slinging his stethoscope around his neck. "Just another little miracle from heaven, I guess."

"Uh-huh." Ty grinned down at Briony. She smiled mistily up at him.

"I'll check in later, but she's going to be fine."

"Thank you, Doctor." Ty stood, stretched, then pulled Briony to her feet and into his arms. One finger laced through the blond curls that clung to her neck and cheek. He stared into her eyes for a long time.

"And thank you. You gave me something I thought I'd lost forever, Briony."

"Your faith was there. You just needed to dig it out and dust it off."

"I don't deserve you," he whispered, face glowing with love. "God knows I don't deserve Cristine, either. But there's no way I'm letting either of you go. You're my life. You make everything good and beautiful again. I love you, Briony Green."

At last he'd said it, on his own, without prodding or fear. Briony spent several long minutes tucking that memory away in her heart. Then she wrapped her arms around him.

"I love you, Tyrel Demens."

"Enough to marry me? Enough to spend whatever time we have together, knowing you'll never have that baby you long for?" His hands cupped her face, his eyes intent as he scrutinized every detail. "Will my love be enough, Briony?"

The joy in her heart suffused her body as she smiled up at him. "Your love is far beyond anything I ever dared dreamed of," she whispered, as the first rays of dawn filled the room with a peach blush. "It's a gift so great, it could only have come from God. I'll spend every day praising Him for allowing me to behold such wonder."

He kissed her, fully and completely, his heart laid

bare. "And you won't mind that we won't share a child?"

The need for reassurance could only be assuaged by her love. Briony knew that. But she knew one thing more.

"Look there, Ty. Look right into this crib and tell me if we don't already have a child, a very blessed baby just waiting for us to love." She saw the pride, relief, love and joy warm his face. "How could we possibly ask for more than Cristine?"

"We couldn't." He nodded as one tear rolled down his craggy cheek. "We couldn't possibly."

"Right." She kissed him quickly, then searched for her bag. From it she withdrew her notepad and a pencil. "Now, we need to start making plans. I've got less than a week till I start my new job, remember? If we're going to get married, I have a couple of friends who insist on being there."

He stared at her. "I forgot about your job. What will you do?"

"I'll move in with you, of course." She grinned at his wide-eyed surprise. "After we're married."

"But—"

"They did say I'd be doing some work in Banff, Ty."

He nodded slowly, his eyes confident, assured. "And after that, we'll just have to trust God." He teased her. "I know you like everything in order and nailed down, but this is one time when your lists won't work, Briony." He grinned at her, his arms tight around her waist. "Marrying me is going to disrupt your life, Professor."

"And yours." She winked. "How do you feel about a wedding next Friday?"

Ty laughed. "I feel pretty good about it." He leaned to whisper in her ear. "I'll marry you any day you want, as long as Cristine is out of here."

"She will be." Briony pulled out her cell phone and dialed, her eyes on the baby's sweet face.

"Clarissa? It's Briony. Can you and Blair come up here? Please?"

"What's wrong?"

Bri snuggled against Ty as happiness overflowed. "I'm planning a wedding," she said. "And I need a little help to make sure this groom doesn't get away."

"Not a chance, sweetheart." Ty held her fast, his eyes shining with love. "Not a chance."

Chapter Fourteen

On the last Friday of June, Bri stood beside Ty and smiled at the dear friends gathered in a mountain glade Ty had chosen especially for their wedding.

"I don't know who to throw my bouquet to," she told Clarissa, smiling as the children raced through the wildflowers, Cristine among them. "You two are already happily married."

"And intending to stay that way, with God's help." Blair patted her swollen tummy, then shook her head at her husband's enquiring look. "Although, if this baby doesn't show up pretty soon, Gabe is going to have a heart attack."

"Gabe will do just fine. We all will. God promised." Clarissa glanced up at the sky and frowned. "I don't like the look of those clouds."

They scurried en masse toward the helicopter Gabe had hired to carry everyone to the secluded wedding.

"Don't worry, it's just a little summer shower. It'll be gone before you know it." Briony watched as Ty scooped up Cristine and strode back toward them. "I feel like I'm dreaming,'' she whispered. ''I don't think I've ever been so happy.''

Clarissa winked at Blair. ''She finished the diary last night.''

''You didn't tell me that.'' Ty helped her over the hillocks, his eyes worried. ''Is everything all right?''

''Everything is perfect.'' She smiled her thanks when Clarissa's husband, Wade, took Cristine. ''I'll tell you all about it later, Ty. But for now, just know that my sister had no qualms about giving her daughter to you. Remember Mrs. King said she saw Bridget by a house?''

He nodded.

''Bridget was watching you play with Cristine. It was the day before she set off to come home to us.'' Bri threw her arms around him and squeezed. ''She knew, Ty, she *knew* Cristine was in the right place, right in your arms, where God wanted her.''

He clutched Bri tightly against his body, whispering words of thanks to the Father who loved his children enough to test them.

''I love you, Briony Demens.''

''I love you, Ty.''

One year later Briony climbed up the last few feet into the glade where she'd been married. Ty lay sprawled out on the grass, softly snoring as the sun beat down on him.

She eased the backpack from her shoulders, then sat down, barely able to contain the love she felt inside.

''You're late.'' Ty's hands slid over her shoulder as his mouth found a sensitive spot on her neck.

''I know. I got held up in Calgary.'' She turned and kissed him back.

"Where's Cristine? Everything all right?" He frowned, staring into her eyes. "Bio-Tek's still standing?"

"Our daughter is with your mother and Giselle. For a few days. Bio-Tek's fine. They're moving more of my stuff out of their office to the building the park service supplied in Banff. We'll start seedlings in the greenhouse soon."

"Good." He gave her a long and satisfying kiss. "I'm so blessed, Briony. You and Cristine are all the family I'll ever need."

"I hope you don't mean that." She held her breath at the glint of pure love shining in his eyes.

"Why?" Ty frowned. "I thought you were happy."

"I am. You know that."

His face tightened; his eyes grew bleak as he fought against the doubts. "But you still wish we had a baby."

She knew the words cost him. He'd worked so hard on his faith, come so far in his trust of God's plan. But it was clear that she'd reminded him of his first wife's desperate need to have a child. Bri rushed to reassure him.

"I love you, Ty. You know that. And I love Cristine. If she's all we ever have, that's more than enough for me."

He frowned. "If?"

Bri found her courage and laid out the facts. "Remember Mrs. King?"

His face wrinkled up in distaste. "The woman from the church group who didn't approve of me or Andrea?"

"That's the one. She caught me just as I was leaving town on my way here."

Ty stared off into the distance, his eyes fixed on the trees he loved to care for. "Oh?"

For a moment Bri was content to sit quietly, surrounded by such vast beauty, content to share it with the man who joined her in her love for this place. Her eyes welled with tears. How great God was. How truly awesome His plans.

"Professor?" Ty snuggled up beside her, his arm around her waist. "What's wrong? Did Mrs. King say something?"

"Oh, yeah. She said something, Tyrel."

He sighed. "We just have to get past it, honey. We're good parents to Cristine. We love her. Eventually Mrs. King will see that."

"Apparently she already has."

"Huh?"

Bri nodded, her heart full to bursting as she gazed into his beloved face.

"Mrs. King has her niece staying with her. The girl needed a place to hide out, people to talk to. You remember the young girl who's been attending our church off and on? She's part of that support group, the one Andrea and Bridget attended."

"That's nice." His thumb brushed the tear off her cheek.

Bri nodded. "It really is, Ty, because Mrs. King says her niece intends to give her baby up for adoption as soon as it's born. Mrs. King says that after watching us with Cristine, her niece believes we'd make the best parents for the child. She wants to know if we're interested."

"*If* we're interested?" He jerked upright. He grabbed Bri's hands, tugged her to her feet and whirled her around. "Of course we're interested. What's with the 'if'?"

Bri hid her smile as he hugged her tight. "She has just one condition," she murmured against his neck, loving the fresh woodsy smell of his clothes.

Her eyes rose to the clear blue sky as realization of the miracle of this gift from the Father welled within. Silently she sent praises winging to heaven.

Ty pressed her away until he could peer into her eyes. "What condition?" he whispered fearfully. Then his face split in a grin of pure delight. "I don't care what condition Mrs. King has, my darling. Why should I? Another child for us can only be a God thing, can't it?"

Bri laughed out loud. "Absolutely," she agreed.

"Then I'd love for us to adopt that blessed baby."

"Well, that's the thing, you see." Bri allowed herself one long minute to savor the peace and trust flooding his countenance. Then she told him.

"It's not 'a' baby."

"It's not a baby?" He frowned, scratched his head and stared. "Then what is it?" He glimpsed the look in her eyes and inhaled sharply. "Twins?" he whispered.

"Nope." Bri shook her head. "Triplets."

Ty sat down. Hard. His face paled, his hands clenched and he gulped for air. "Three babies?" His eyes begged her to explain.

Bri chuckled as she plunked down beside him and placed her hand in his. "Mrs. King just found out, too. I think she's in as much shock as you."

"No wonder!"

"Anyway, her niece is undergoing a C-section in about three hours. The doctors feel it's time. The babies will be early, but apparently they're healthy enough and should do very well.''

"But—the mother? Is she certain about her decision? Her aunt isn't pushing her?''

Bri's heart warmed at the thought that this big man could be more concerned about the needs of a pregnant teenager than his own wants and desires.

''Apparently she decided not to have an abortion after Mrs. King offered her a place to stay, but she's always maintained that she wouldn't keep the child. They got talking about Bridget a few months ago. Once she heard Bridget's story, she began to watch Cristine.'' Bri shook her head at her own stupidity.

''They've been past our place a lot on their 'walks,' but I didn't realize why. Mrs. King said seeing Cristine, and the love we have for her, decided the issue.'' She hugged close to his side.

''She's only seventeen, Ty, and desperately afraid that her babies won't have a home to go to, that they'll end up in some government care, separated, unloved. She *wants* us to have them. Us!''

Ty squeezed his eyes closed. A tear rolled down his cheek. When he finally spoke, his hushed voice touched her heart.

''I give up, God,'' he said on a broken sob. ''I don't understand You, I'm not sure if I ever will, but thank You.''

Briony touched his chin, tilted it up, unable to withhold her joy one minute longer. ''Babies, Ty. He's giving us three blessed babies to add to our family.''

''Sons,'' he breathed, his fingers grazing her cheeks as the tears rolled down. His face changed, softened. ''Or more beautiful daughters?''

''I don't know, Ty. We're supposed to go to Calgary

right away. If we hurry, we might even see them born.''

"Born? Oh, my!" He peered down at Bri. "I'm going to be a father again," he said in stunned surprise.

She giggled. "Yes, darling. I know."

The impact of God's tender care flooded over them as the soft afternoon air swept across the glade.

"'Before they ask, I will answer.'" Ty's whisper brushed across her hair.

"He had it all planned, Ty. He knew exactly what He was doing, every step of the way. His ways are perfect and right and just."

"I'm only just beginning to understand that." Ty hugged her close. "Don't let me forget, Bri, will you?"

"We'll remind each other," she said firmly. "And every single day we'll remind our children how blessed we are to have a Father who loves us more than we can possibly imagine. Maybe someday it will help them to trust Him."

"You are one very smart scientist, Prof." He kissed her. "I don't believe I've told you half often enough."

Bri grinned. "You can tell me now."

Ty shook his head, his eyes filled with love as he pulled her upright, then led her across the meadow.

"Not now. Maybe later."

"Why not now?" She pouted.

"Because right now we have to go welcome our kids into God's world." His mouth curved with delight. "Come on, Mama."

Bri trotted at his side, her heart full. All of this because of Bridget's blessed baby!

"You're too quiet," Ty said later as he drove down

the road toward Calgary, toward the future. "What's going on?"

"I'm making up a list—"

"Uh, Professor?"

"Yes?"

"Just this once, let's forget your list. God never follows it, anyway." His eyes shone with a joy too big to be contained. "Why don't you snuggle up next to me and we'll remind each other of our blessings?"

"Okay," she whispered.

And she did.

*   *   *   *   *

Dear Reader,

Thanks so much for picking up this third book in the **IF WISHES WERE WEDDINGS** series. I hope that, with me, you began to see ways in your own life in which God turned bad into good, made joy out of sadness, answered before we could even form the question.

Day after day I find new things about Him, new ways to catch a glimpse of a God who so loves me He would go far out of His way to work His pleasure in my life.

May you find your life blessed by the often quiet, gentle brush of His fingers over the pages of your life and may you hear His sweet voice in the midst of life's biggest uncertainties.

Blessings to you,

Next Month
From Steeple Hill's

Love Inspired

A GROOM WORTH WAITING FOR

by *Crystal Stovall*

Jilted at the altar by her fiancé, Amy Jenkins vows to start a new life in Lexington, Kentucky. But her plans go terribly awry when she's held up in a convenience store robbery! Having survived the attack thanks to a dynamic stranger, she finds herself drawn deeply into Matthew Wynn's life. Does God's plan for her future include finding in Matthew a groom worth waiting for?

Don't miss
A GROOM WORTH WAITING FOR
On sale November 2001

Visit us at www.steeplehill.com
LIAGWWF